The Music Plays Past Midnight
Marilyn Cram Donahue

Chariot Books

This book is for
Margaret
who makes music
wherever she goes.

Chariot Books is an imprint of David C. Cook Publishing
David C. Cook Publishing Co., Elgin, Illinois 60120
David C. Cook Publishing Co., Weston, Ontario

THE MUSIC PLAYS PAST MIDNIGHT
© 1983 by Marilyn Cram Donahue

Cover design by James A. Zitzman, Jr.
Cover photo by Robert Cushman Hayes

Printed in the United States of America
89 88 87 86 85 84 83   5 4 3 2 1

Library of Congress Cataloging in Publication Data

Donahue, Marilyn Cram.
    The music plays past midnight.

    (Chariot books)
    Summary: Caro, believing herself lacking in the talents she
sees in others, finds her days boring until she realizes the gift of
friendship is as great a talent as any other.
    [1. Friendship—Fiction] I. Title.
PZ7.D71475Mu 1983   [Fic]   83-70900
ISBN 0-89191-756-X

Contents

1
Sappy Syl

The little bell in the restaurant door rang when Caro opened it. She quickly stepped inside and kicked the door shut behind her.

"You're early," said Flo, peering through the side doorway that led into Second Chance, the used clothing shop that connected to the Original Maria's restaurant. Flo owned both places and hired Caro to help her for a couple of hours after school each day and for three hours every Saturday morning. "I was about to have a cup of coffee. Care to join me?"

Caro grinned and nodded. It was always the same. Every Friday Flo invited her to have an afternoon cup of coffee with her—mostly milk because Flo said she didn't cotton to twelve-year-old kids drinking the stuff black.

"I think you have a visitor, Caro." Flo nodded toward the front window.

Caro didn't have to look back. She knew who it was. Syl had been bugging her all day at school, and she was going to bug her now. Each Friday, Syl followed Caro home to Bundy Street, then stood outside the restaurant, looking in the window.

Caro ignored Flo's comment and purposely changed the subject. "I smell hot tamales."

"That's nothing new. This place always smells like hot tamales." Flo laughed and waved her arm. "Help yourself, honey. You know where the kitchen is as well as I do." Flo did all the cooking at Maria's herself, and people came all the way from downtown to taste her food. The crowd was always gone by one o'clock, and they left a real mess behind them. It was Caro's job to finish cleaning up on weekdays, but on Saturday mornings she got to help Flo cook. Caro could make a pretty good tamale. Even Flo said so.

As Caro walked to the back of the restaurant she smiled at the few Friday afternoon regulars who were seated at small tables. She went right to the kitchen counter and began to peel the corn-husk wrapping away from a tamale. The soft cornmeal and the hot, spicy filling was always a good after-school snack.

Caro sat down at the rickety kitchen table and Flo joined her. "I think you have a visitor, Caro," Flo said again.

"Yuck!" Caro exclaimed. "I'll never escape her!"

"Why do you want to?"

"Because she's a creep."

Mary Ruth Jefferson had called her that. She had called Syl several other things, too. At school Mary Ruth only went around with kids she considered "preppy." Those were the ones who got invited to her parties. Caro hadn't been invited yet, but she was working on it.

In her mind Caro could see Syl, her face pressed against the front window until she looked like a fish with a flat nose and pushed-in lips and bulging eyes. Caro could even see the pimples—little tiny ones that

6

looked like miniature red ants. Syl's cousin, Took (his real name was Arnold Tooker, but if you called him that he would punch you) said that when Syl used to talk real loud and fast, it looked as if the red ants were crawling all over her face.

Syl didn't talk loud and fast anymore, and Caro knew the reason why. Took had told Caro's sister, Angie. It was because of Syl's size. She was little. Really little. She was so little her teeth looked too big for the rest of her.

"If you don't grow pretty soon, you'll turn out to be a midget," all the kids taunted her.

Took said Syl had gone home one day and asked her mother why she was so small; her mother had told her she was little because she talked so loud and fast. Using up all her strength on her voice didn't leave any energy for growing. So Syl had stopped talking. She hardly ever said anything at all and when she did, she whispered.

Caro sighed. She pushed her chair back and looked helplessly at Flo. "I suppose I'll have to go out there and talk to her," she said. "It won't take long because she never says much of anything back."

"Why not invite her in? There are more hot tamales back here than an army could eat."

Caro stared at Flo. Invite Syl to come in—right in here where Caro and Flo were sitting and enjoying each other? It was out of the question. Caro shook her head. "Nobody ever invites her anywhere."

As soon as the words were out of her mouth, Caro knew she had made a mistake. Flo was a sucker for stray dogs and cats and people nobody wanted. Right now she was giving Caro one of those you-ought-to-know-better-than-that looks.

"I'm going—I'm going," she said. "But don't say I didn't warn you."

She hurried back up front and pushed open the door

7

of Maria's. "Hey, Syl," she called. "Flo says you can come in if you want to."

Syl sidled along the sidewalk, scooted in front of Caro, and slipped quickly through the restaurant and into the chair next to Flo's. Once she saw Caro's tamale across the table, she never took her eyes off it.

Flo smiled and put one arm around Syl's skinny shoulders. She was always putting her arm around somebody. That was the kind of person she was. "Join us in a little snack?" she asked.

Syl nodded and sniffed hungrily. Flo got up and went to the sink. Caro could hardly believe it. Sappy Syl was going to sit right across the table from her, and she would have to watch her while she ate. Caro had seen Syl's table manners in the cafeteria at school and they weren't anything you'd want a repeat performance of.

Flo came back with a large tray holding two plates and forks, a pitcher of milk, and a platter of hot tamales. Before she could finish setting it on the table, Syl was helping herself—peeling off the wrappings with both hands and shoveling the food into her mouth. Caro didn't think she chewed anything—just swallowed it in great gulps. When Flo said, "Hey, there! You'd better slow down, honey," Syl's eyes got bigger and she ate faster.

As soon as she was finished, she hiccuped once, wiped her mouth on her bare arm, and stood up. She made a beeline for the front door without so much as a "thank-you" or "good-bye."

"See," Caro said. "What did I tell you? She really is a creep."

Flo shook her head. "Poor little thing. She doesn't have any manners at all. It's funny, too, because her sister has more than she needs."

"Jessica?" Caro gave a snort. "She really likes to pretend she's somebody. But it's all a put-on!" She

8

hesitated. "Jessica's not so bad when you get to know her."

"Maybe somebody should get to know Syl. . ."

"Maybe, but don't look at me. I just wish she would stop trailing me around as if I have something she wants."

Flo looked at her a minute, one eyebrow raised high. "There must be a reason she picked you," she said. Then she got up and began to stack the dirty dishes.

Flo never was one to beat around the bush. "It's not like you to be mean to people, Caro. Last week, you almost bit Took's head off. Yesterday, you were downright rude to your mother. And here you are today, turning your back on someone who looks up to you."

Caro laughed. "It's not hard to be mean to Took. He's the kind of person who invites insults." She saw the corner of Flo's mouth turn up and knew she understood, even if she didn't approve.

"I don't know what made me say those things to mom yesterday," she told Flo. "I didn't mean them. But it seems as if she doesn't listen to me anymore. She's always lying down and resting and telling me she'll talk to me later."

Caro stopped and thought about her mother, remembering how hard she had worked to keep the family together, how they had hardly ever seen her, and how she and Angie had been afraid they would have to go and live with their Great-aunt Martha in Massachusetts. That was before her mother and Tony had gotten married. Now life had changed for all of them. Caro felt ashamed. There must be a reason for the way her mother had been acting lately.

But Syl was getting to be a real problem, and Caro thought she had finally figured out the reason why. "I . . . guess I can't stand Syl because she's so little and unimportant."

Flo didn't say a word or look at Caro—just put a stack of dishes into a sinkful of hot, soapy water and handed her a towel. The silence made Caro uncomfortable. She knew Flo didn't approve of what she had said.

After a minute, she added, "Oh, I know. It's not easy to be a dud. . . ." She dried a glass and put it in the cupboard. "I guess I know how Syl feels. I feel like one, too, sometimes." Caro wasn't sure why she'd admitted that to Flo; she had never told anyone else how she felt. "What I mean is," Caro added before Flo would think Caro really was a dud, "—everyone seems so important. Like Angie, who helped Con after his legs had to be amputated.

"And Con. He walks on artificial legs and never complains. . . . But I never do anything that anybody's going to remember. I go to school, come home, and help a little in the store. That's it."

Flo let the water out of the sink, rinsed her hands, and dried them. "You feel like a little fish in a big pond. Is that it?"

"Yeah, that's just about it." Suddenly inspired, Caro added, "Or like a chicken in a nest of gorgeous sea gulls! I want people to look at me and smile and think how special I am. But they don't, because all I do is peck around the coop and hope I won't end up on somebody's dinner table." Caro thought of Mary Ruth Jefferson and the way she and her friends made fun of the other girls' clothes: "Where'd you get that?" they'd say. "At the K-Mart?" Caro was always sure she'd be the next to be ridiculed.

Flo began to laugh. Scowling, Caro looked up at her. But Flo's laughter was contagious. Caro smiled in spite of herself.

"Honey," Flo declared, "you'll never end up on anybody's dinner table. You're too tough. Now wait a minute," she said as Caro started to protest. "I'm talking about a good kind of tough. You may only be twelve years old, but you can see things the way they are."

Caro thought that last part was probably true. She didn't believe in pretending. What was the use? You had to look at the world the way it really was.

Flo reached over and took Caro's face between her hands. She planted a kiss right in the middle of Caro's forehead, then let her go. "You're good with people, Caro, but you haven't been acting like it lately."

Caro looked at her suspiciously. "Are you talking about Syl?"

Flo shrugged. "It wouldn't take much to make the child happy, and you would hardly notice the effort it takes to say hello."

Caro wasn't so sure about that. She didn't think Syl would be satisfied that easily. "Suppose she starts hanging around every day? Friday is bad enough."

"That's something you'll have to figure out for yourself," Flo told her. "Right now, you're worried about feeling unimportant. . . . Did you ever think that the things that are hardest to do might be the most important, Caro?"

Caro had to be honest. She shook her head hard. To tell the truth, she wanted to think about Syl as little as possible. *I feel enough like a dud, myself,* she thought, *without being friends with Syl and letting everybody know I'm a dud.*

The front door opened and closed and Flo had to go and wait on the customers. Lots of people came in late Friday afternoon and ordered hot tamales to go, which meant that Caro would pack them in aluminum trays and wrap them tightly in foil packages. Sometimes they also ordered Flo's special guacamole or her home-made tortillas or trays of enchiladas that were filled with onions and olives and smothered with rich red sauce and cheese. Before Caro knew it, it was time for

11

the dinner crowd to arrive. This meant that Amy Chou, from Hoang Chou's Laundry down the street, came in to help serve, and Caro went home.

Caro walked along Bundy Street past the old green apartment house where they used to live. It was growing dark outside, and the building seemed dusted with shadows. There was a bare place now where the morning-glory vine had been. It had grown thick on each side of the front steps, clinging to the mortuary pillars that decorated the shabby entrance. The vine had seeded like a weed in a sidewalk crack the summer of Con's terrible accident. It had bloomed once, then scattered its seeds so that the next year tiny plants sprang up all along Bundy Street.

It was the last part of January now. In a few months, Caro thought, there would be flowers from one end of Bundy Street to the other. That was one of the joys of living in California.

She passed Hoang Chou's Laundry, which was closed but still smelled of steam, and Chico's Cabin, which was open and smelled of hamburgers and barbecue smoke. She crossed at Chico's corner, hurried past the Universal Mission with its statue of George Washington covered with gold paint, and arrived breathless at Tony's Deli.

Caro was glad to be home. She loved it here where they all lived together in the back rooms, and she loved her whole, mixed-up happy family: Tony and her mother; her sister, Angie; Con, who had come to live with them after the accident; and little Bandit, Tony's monkey. As Caro opened the door she could hear laughter coming from the rooms in back.

She slammed the door behind her and heard the little bell ring. "Hi, everybody! I'm home!" she called. But nobody seemed to hear her. And when she went into the back rooms and stood in the doorway, not one person noticed that she was there.

2
Such a Blessing!

Caro watched her family a minute before she went slowly into the big room. Angie was setting the table. It was long and rectangular and had once stood in the reference room of the downtown library. Caro loved the way the grain of the wood swirled on the oak surface like currents of a river. So did her mother. That's why they used place mats—so the wood could still be seen. But tonight there was a white cloth on the table and yellow flowers in a blue bowl and candles burning in brass holders on the buffet.

Caro's mother was already seated in her place, and Con was sitting next to her, his crutches leaning against the back of his chair and Con himself leaning forward holding both her mother's hands in his. Tony was standing by her mother, his arm on her shoulder, and he couldn't have looked more pleased if he had just been elected president. His bushy black mustache accentuated the smile on his face. Bandit was safe in his cage, but his little eyes were round with surprise and he was chattering shrilly in response to all the excitement.

Everyone seemed to be talking at once but nobody made any sense. "So wonderful! I can't believe it! Oh Tony! Oh Evelyn! Have to think of a name! What a surprise! What a blessing! What a . . ."

"Hold it!"

Caro was surprised at the sound of her own voice. Now why had she said that? She could have walked in and kissed her mother and quietly asked what was going on. That's what any normal person would have done. She saw herself in the mirror above the buffet. Her face seemed very white. But the flames from the candles seemed to make her freckles more obvious and her hair brighter than ever. It was red hair, thick and curly, so that her mother cut it short and close to her head. Flo always said it was the color of a summer sunset, but Took had once told her that it was more like mustard and catsup all squished together on a hot dog after you'd taken the first bite.

Everyone stopped talking. Even Bandit closed his mouth. It was as if someone had pulled a plug. "I'm sorry," she said. "I . . . I didn't mean to yell like that. But you were all talking so fast."

"Really, Caro," her mother began, but Tony leaned over and whispered something and she looked up at him and smiled. Tony had that kind of effect on people. He could calm them down and keep them from saying things they would be sorry for later. Tony listened when you talked to him. When you asked him questions, he gave you honest answers. Caro wished she could talk to him now, without everybody standing around listening.

As if he had read her mind, Tony reached out his free arm to Caro and pulled her close. "We are the ones who should be sorry," he told her. "We should have waited until you got home, Caro, but we were so excited that the news just seemed to spill out."

"What news? What's happening?"

She saw the way her mother glanced up at Tony. Her fair skin was flushed, and she looked . . . well, radiant was the best word Caro could think of. Con was grinning from ear to ear, and Angie was holding a fork in midair, watching the rest of them expectantly.

It was her mother who told her. "It's good news, Caro. The most wonderful news. We just came from the doctor's office, and he told us what we wanted to hear. Our family is growing—we're going to have a baby!"

"A baby?" That was impossible. Her mother's hair was still light brown, not even graying at the temples, but certainly she was too old to have a baby.

"Isn't that wonderful? That's why we're celebrating tonight."

"You . . . and Tony?" Caro felt like covering her face with her hands and dropping dead on the floor. How medieval of them. Caro couldn't believe they would consider such a thing. What would people think?

"Well, of course. I hope you're as happy as we are."

Caro stared at her mother a minute. She had been brought up to tell the truth—at all costs. But if she told it now, there would be a scene nobody would forget.

"Absolutely," she lied. "It's a . . . big surprise."

How would she ever face Mary Ruth? How would she face any of the kids in Mary Ruth's crowd? She could hear them now. "A baby! You can't be serious, Caro!" And then they would titter and talk behind her back. "Hey, have you heard about Caro's mother and Tony, the organ-grinder?" And then they would whisper things about overpopulation and poor people having poor ways.

Tony reached out right then and gave her a giant

hug. She hugged him back, gratefully burying her face in his shirt, hoping nobody could tell what was going on in her mind. Everybody in the family was happy except her. What was the matter with them? Couldn't they see how this was going to look to other people? Couldn't they see how embarrassing it was? Besides, who needed a baby? Everything had been wonderful the way it was. And now there would be this extra person getting in the way.

Caro looked across the room and saw herself in the mirror again. Caro Rafferty: a displaced person. Even if she saved someone's life or won a contest or got all A's at school (which wasn't likely), nobody would think Caro was important. This nameless, faceless, sexless question mark of a baby was crowding her out. For the first time since her mother had married Tony, Caro felt like an outsider. She felt as if her mother had handed her her coat and said, "Nice to have known you."

Her mother gave her a quizzical look, then quickly reached out and pulled her onto her lap the way she used to in the old days. She hugged her and ruffled her hair, and then she groaned as she always did and said, "You're just about too big for me to hold, aren't you?"

Caro didn't answer. She had always laughed before, but tonight it didn't seem funny. Her mother squeezed her once more. "Help Angie get dinner on the table, will you, sweetie?"

Caro nodded and got up without a word. She hadn't belonged on her mother's lap for a long time. She stumbled on the braided rug and almost fell but nobody noticed, except Angie, who had been watching her from the kitchen. "Are you all right?" she whispered.

Caro nodded again. "Why wouldn't I be?"

"Well, you don't look all right. You're as white as a sheet. Maybe you're coming down with something."

Caro thought that sounded like a good idea. It would

be nice to crawl into bed and close her eyes and pull the covers right up to her nose. She hadn't done that for a long time. It didn't work, she had decided. Your problems were always right there waiting for you when you came out again. But just the same, she felt like doing it tonight.

"Caro . . ." Her mother was calling to her. "Maybe you can help us think of some names for the baby. You're usually good at that sort of thing."

Caro didn't answer until Angie kicked her in the shin. "Yeah . . . sure," she said. "I'll be thinking about it."

She was glad when they started carrying the food to the table and she had something to do besides stand around and get in the way. Generally she liked to work with Angie in the kitchen. But Angie was working fast tonight, and Caro's world seemed to be turning in slow motion.

Finally, they were all seated at the table and Tony was asking the blessing. Caro thought he would never get through. Most nights he gave thanks for the food and for the fellowship and let it go at that. But tonight he waxed eloquent. He talked so much about the blessed event that anyone would have thought he had never had a baby before. With a shock, Caro realized that it was true. This was Tony Genovese's first baby. She wished she knew why this whole thing made her so uncomfortable.

After dinner, she and Angie did the dishes. Angie was getting prettier and prettier, Caro thought. She was tall like all the Raffertys. She had straight, brown hair, but she didn't pull it back tight with a rubber band anymore. She curled it with the electric iron Tony had gotten her for Christmas. She and Con made a nice couple. So did Caro's mother and Tony. And that left Caro.

She went to bed as soon as possible and pulled the

covers up to her nose and closed her eyes tight. She didn't want to think. She didn't want to dream. But she did dream—the old dream that frightened her—the dream that made her remember when she was back at the old place across the street—in the tiny downstairs apartment where she and Angie slept together in the hard, little bed that dropped down out of the living room wall.

It had been lonesome there, with her mother sleeping days and working nights and Angie gone a lot of the time. Lots of times Caro had been scared, but she hadn't told anybody. Now, when she dreamed about it, that part of her life seemed real again and Caro was scared, just as she had been so many times before.

When Caro opened her eyes, it was morning, and she felt as tired as if she had lived those terrible days over again. She raised her head and looked slowly and fearfully around her room, almost ready to believe that the old days were still with her. But Angie was sound asleep in her own bed by the window, and Caro could see a shaft of sunlight slanting across the flowered wallpaper that she had chosen herself as a surprise for Angie's birthday.

She stretched her toes under the covers and remembered that this was Saturday. That it was two whole years since Con's accident. That her mother had married Tony, and they had all moved into the rooms at the back of the Deli where Caro could smell hot pastrami and fresh bread twenty-four hours a day and have a giant dill pickle out of the crock whenever she wanted it—free!

Then she remembered the baby, and she turned over and groaned.

"What's the matter? Are you sick?" Angie raised up on one elbow and peered at her. "You sure have been crabby lately. Is something bothering you?"

Caro wanted to say, "Yeah, I feel like a chicken—

peck, peck, peck." But she said instead, "I was thinking about that dumb Syl. It's Saturday, and I'll bet she'll hang around all day."

"Why don't you try being nice to her for a change?"

Caro didn't think that deserved an answer. She had been nice to Syl yesterday and what good had it done? It hadn't improved Syl's manners any.

She climbed out of bed and pulled on her jeans. She was going to have some cheese and a giant dill pickle for breakfast, then go straight to work at Flo's. Making tamales might not change the world, but it was something nobody else in her family knew how to do. She would make piles of them today—enough to feed the city. But she didn't intend to offer any free samples to Syl. That would be a waste of perfectly good food.

3
A Scared
Alley Cat

It was almost noon before Syl showed up. She stood around outside, pressing her face against the big window and watching the early customers eat lunch.

"Look at that!" Caro exclaimed. "She's going to ruin your business, Flo. Nobody wants to eat with a creep like that staring at them."

"I expect she's staring at the food," Flo said. "But the customers may not know that. You better go out there, Caro, and ask her to come in."

"You've got to be kidding. Why don't I just send her packing?"

Flo didn't answer at first. Then she said softly, "You might feel a lot better about yourself, Caro, if you tried some little acts of kindness. You can't fly like a sea gull if you don't begin with the little things. Not trying is the only way you can really be a failure."

Caro wasn't sure that being kind to Syl would help

her "fly like a sea gull"; certainly Mary Ruth Jefferson wouldn't agree with Flo. But Caro knew better than to disregard Flo's wishes. She went to the front door, fuming all the way. The next thing she knew, Flo would be trying to teach Syl to make tamales—as if the kid had sense enough to learn.

"Flo says you can come in," she said. Syl slithered through the doorway and headed for the kitchen, but Caro caught her by the shirttail. It was a boy's shirt she was wearing, and for one crazy moment Caro thought it was the same one Took used to wear every day until his mother finally broke down and bought him a new one.

"Listen," Caro hissed, "if Flo is nice enough to let you in here, you'd better mind your manners. That means saying 'Please,' and 'Thank you,' and not running off like a scared alley cat. Have you got that?"

Syl gave her a smile that showed a broken front tooth. She didn't make a sound, but her head was going up and down, so she must have understood.

"And another thing—you can't go back in the kitchen where the food is until you clean yourself up."

Syl looked down at her grubby hands. She seemed surprised. It occurred to Caro that she didn't even know she was dirty. Caro sighed. "Come on. I'll show you how."

She pushed open the rest room door. Luckily, there was nobody else in there. Caro sure wouldn't have wanted an audience while she scrubbed Syl. She turned on the tap and waited until the water was hot. "Roll up your sleeves," she ordered. Then she held up a bar of soap. "When you put this stuff on wet skin, it makes the dirt come off."

Syl didn't move. She looked at Caro trustingly. *Just like a puppy that nobody wants,* Caro thought. There was a strange lump forming at the back of her throat, and she swallowed it away. If she had a puppy, she wouldn't let it get like this. She plunged Syl's hands and arms into the warm water and watched the suds turn brown. Little bits of dead skin began to roll away like dark eraser crumbs from white paper.

"How long has it been since you took a bath?" Caro demanded. Syl looked up at her and shrugged. "Doesn't your mother make you bathe?" Syl looked down at the sink of soapy water and whispered something Caro couldn't hear. "Speak up, Syl," Caro said as she rubbed harder.

"Ouch, that hurts," Syl whispered. Caro rinsed the arms and saw that she had scrubbed them until they were a bright, splotchy pink.

"Sorry," she said. "But you were so dirty, Syl, that I didn't think it would ever come off. Now let's do your face."

Syl gave her a horrified look and grabbed for the soap. "I can do it," she mouthed.

Caro stepped back to watch, glad she wasn't going to have to touch those pimples. She was surprised to see Syl showing so much spunk. But that didn't mean she could be trusted. Caro intended to stand right there until she was clean enough for Flo's kitchen. Caro watched until the face was washed and dried. She inspected it carefully and made Syl wash and dry it again.

"OK," she finally said. "I guess you'll do. But I'll bet the rest of you needs the same treatment."

She led the way back to the kitchen where Flo was elbow deep in flour. Stacks of fresh, hot tortillas lined the counter. Refried beans bubbled gently in a huge pot. Great colanders were overflowing with shredded lettuce and cheese, and there were big bowls of sliced tomatoes, black olives, and homemade chili salsa. Enchiladas on large, shallow trays sat on racks, ready for the oven. Tamales were steaming on the stove. And Flo had already fried a batch of taco tortillas, crisp and

22

folded, ready for stuffing.

Caro knew that more tamales needed to be made. These were the favorites, and there were hardly ever enough. She motioned for Syl to get out of the way, and when she didn't move, Caro nudged her over to the side of the kitchen where Flo kept a tall, three-legged stool at the end of the counter. "You can sit over there out of the way. Don't bother us, because we're going to be busy."

Syl climbed up onto the stool. Her eyes grew so big at the sight of all that food that Caro thought they were going to pop. But Syl didn't make a sound—except for one long, loud sniff that could be heard all over the kitchen. Caro thought it was as if Syl were trying to suck in all the good smells and keep them there. She wondered if Syl had had anything to eat since Flo fed her last.

"Hungry?" Flo asked, as if she had been thinking the same thing.

Syl looked at Caro and hesitated. Then she looked down at her hands and shook her head.

"Don't look at me like that, Flo," Caro protested. "I just told her not to bother us. I'm not trying to starve her or anything. Gee whiz! If I hadn't cleaned her up, you wouldn't have let her in your kitchen."

"I appreciate that, Caro. You did a good job. Now let's fix a nice big plate, shall we?"

Caro knew what "we" meant. It meant "Caro." Well, it wasn't any skin off her back if Flo wanted to give all her food away. She took a small plate out of the cupboard, glanced at Flo, and decided she'd better get a bigger one. She piled it high, omitting nothing. Nobody was going to accuse her of trying to starve that kid. She put the full plate down in front of Syl and gave her a fork.

"You can pick up the taco in your fingers," she said, "but not the rest. Now look, Syl, here's a napkin. Wipe your mouth on this, not your arms. And don't eat so fast!"

There was a look on Syl's face that Caro didn't want to see—a kind of mixture of fear and excitement. She could understand the excitement. Flo's food was wonderful. But what did Syl have to be afraid of? They lived in a nice house with a little garden, and their mother was a secretary and made plenty of money. Syl's sister, Jessica, talked about it all the time. She was always telling everybody about the special meals their mother cooked. She only bought the best, Jess said, and they went places together on the weekends and had a great time. It sounded to Caro as if Syl and Jessica had it made. So why did Syl look so scared, and why was she hungry all the time?

Caro didn't have time to think about it now. She was too busy spreading cornmeal on husks, adding the filling, then rolling the tamales up and tying the ends tightly. She looked up once and saw Syl eating. When she saw Caro watching her, she picked up her napkin and wiped her mouth.

The next time Caro looked, Syl's plate was empty, and she was sitting there looking glassy-eyed. Caro couldn't believe it. There had been enough on that plate to feed three. At least she was sitting over there quietly and not bothering anybody. Caro could almost stand her when she was full and quiet and at least partly clean. She would let her sit there a few more minutes, and then she would tell her it was time for her to go home.

But Flo had other plans. "Come on over here, honey, and learn something useful," she said.

For a few horrible seconds Caro thought Flo was going to teach Syl her tamale secrets. Nobody but Flo and Caro knew those. But when she saw what Flo had in mind, she relaxed. Sprinkling grated cheese on tacos and adding a black olive wouldn't hurt anything.

Even Syl could handle that. To Caro's surprise, she handled it pretty well. She was neat and quick—and she liked what she was doing so much that her broken tooth showed almost all the time. Caro found herself wondering what Syl would be like if she took a bath and washed her hair and put on clean clothes.

When it was time for Caro to go, she waved to Flo and slipped out the kitchen door. Flo nodded and waved back. Syl didn't even turn around. Caro hurried through the dining room and out the front door. She didn't relax until she was at Chico's corner and ready to cross on the green light. She figured she had been a pretty good sport all morning, but enough was enough. She didn't intend to have Syl on her tail all afternoon, too.

Tony was waiting for her. He had taken Bandit out of his cage and had fastened the leather rope to the metal loop on the little monkey's collar. Tony's hand organ was standing against the wall, its dark, polished wood shining against a border of yellow roses. Bandit was hopping excitedly, and Caro didn't blame him. He loved the music of the organ. Sometimes Caro thought he wanted it to play forever so that the monkey could endlessly dance and perform and tip his hat. Tony's music had a happy sound. It made you feel free.

The Genoveses had always been organ-grinders. Hurdy-gurdy men. It was a family tradition, and Tony's hand organ had passed on from father to son for generations. It was like a giant music box on wheels. Tony could push it wherever he wanted, and there was a tiny compartment where Bandit could ride. Tony made his living from the Deli, because he said he couldn't pay his bills with pennies. But he still loved to grind the organ and make people smile. He and Bandit used to go to Chinatown on Saturday nights and to La Mirada Beach every Sunday afternoon, but Tony had been busy lately, and he hadn't taken Bandit out

25

much. Now here he was, ready to go, and it was only Saturday afternoon.

"Why not?" Tony asked. "It's fun to do something unexpected, and I feel like going to the beach today."

Caro wondered what her mother would say and was surprised when she came out from the back rooms smiling. "Have a good time, you two—I mean, you three. It's a beautiful day for going to the beach."

"Sure you don't want to come along, Evelyn?" Tony asked.

"Not this time. But I'll have something good for dinner when you get back."

She leaned over and gave Caro a kiss, and Caro knew that she did want to go. Her mother loved the beach. But she was staying home so that Caro could go alone with Tony. Her mother was a special kind of person.

They let Bandit ride on Tony's shoulder until the bus arrived at Chico's corner. Then Tony opened the little door in the organ cart, and Bandit jumped inside. Caro felt like singing. Ever since the day when Angie had taken her to La Mirada two years ago, it had been her favorite place in the whole world. There was a huge beach, with white, white sand that stretched for miles along broad sidewalks where people skated or rode their bikes. But the best thing was the pier—a real carnival pier with a carousel and games and places to buy cotton candy and hamburgers and corn dogs and fried fish in a basket, and chips as thick as two thumbs.

At La Mirada, you could ride the merry-go-round for a quarter while the music played, "My Darling Clementine" and "The Sidewalks of New York." And when you got tired of riding, you could walk along the pier and still hear the music, even above the sounds of the ocean. The fishermen said if the organ broke, they wouldn't catch any more fish. Then, they said, they would have to hire Tony full time, just to keep the music going.

Caro settled down in her favorite seat in the back of the bus. It wasn't far to La Mirada, but it took twenty minutes to get there because of the traffic. She had never gone by herself, but she thought she was old enough. That was one of the things she would talk to Tony about today.

She sighed happily as she heard the bus give the *whooshing* sound that meant it was ready to start. Then she thought she heard something else. A voice calling her name. She turned in her seat and looked out the back window.

"Caarrro," came a wailing cry, all the way down Bundy Street.

It was Syl. She must have come out of Flo's just in time to see them getting on the bus. She was running fast, trying to catch up. She had almost reached Chico's Alley when the bus started to move across the intersection. She slowed down and stopped at the corner, watching it go.

There wasn't anything she could do about it, Caro told herself. Anyway, she didn't want Syl tagging along with her and Tony today. She turned back around in her seat and began to count the streets as they passed by: Fiftieth, Forty-Ninth, Forty-Eighth . . . When they reached Third Street, they would get off and walk to the ocean.

They were almost there when Caro realized that Syl had shouted her name. Really shouted it. Out loud.

4
The Pier People

Caro pulled the cord at Third Street, and she and Tony got off at the top of the hill. It was only a short walk past the little beach cottages with their bright gardens down to the beach itself, where the sand spread for miles and the deep blue ocean seemed to reach to eternity.

They turned left and walked along the broad sidewalk next to the sand. The pier was ahead, rising above the beach and stretching out toward the sea. It cast a long shadow where children liked to play in the sand, then continued far out over the water, held high on tall wooden posts called piles. They were like telephone poles, Caro thought, with their ends sunk firmly into the sand of the beach and the bottom of the sea.

People were walking beneath the pier, strolling along the sand, and farther out Caro could see the fishermen leaning out over the water to cast their lines. She took a deep breath and let the fresh, salty air go clear to the bottom of her lungs. She watched a sea gull swoop low over the pier and snatch a small fish from a fisherman's basket. Then the bird glided high into the air and out over the water, flapping its wings once, as if to say, "Try to stop me!"

There aren't any chickens at La Mirada Beach, Caro thought. The knowledge made her feel joyful and free.

She followed Tony up the cement steps to the top of the pier. Just ahead, on their left, was the carousel, housed in a big red building that would have been like a barn, except that it was so fancy. There were dozens of tall, narrow doorways with bright yellow arches. Above these, mullioned windows covered the upper level, resting above an ornately curved molding that went all the way around the building.

Four square towers sat on each corner, with more windows that seemed to be lookouts. Above the building, the roof sloped steeply, rising to form a huge inverted funnel with a circular vent on top. The whole roof was made of metal and painted silver so that it gleamed in the sunlight. The building looked like a great red fortress or like a castle with a silver cap on top.

A long boardwalk stretched from the carousel along one side of the pier where brightly decorated game booths, tiny shops, and food stands stood. At the far end, over deep water, was a bait and tackle shop, the harbor master's office, and steep wooden stairs that led down to a lower level just above the water. Here, people came to rent boats, arrange for sailing lessons, or eat at Sinbad's—the little cafe that specialized in breakfasts, hamburgers, and BLT's.

Tony opened the little door of Bandit's compartment. Bandit squealed excitedly and leaped to the ground, running the length of his rope and back again. Then he gave a jump onto Tony's arm and from there to his shoulder, where he sat, chattering happily.

"Let's take a little walk first," Tony said. Caro knew what he meant. As soon as Tony started the music, the crowd would gather. Tony would become the hurdy-gurdy man, and they wouldn't have a chance to talk again until Bandit disappeared into his box at the end of the day.

They walked together all the way to the end of the pier, far out over the water. The waves rose and fell in a gentle rhythm today, slapping gently against the tall wooden piles that stood like giant, barnacle-covered stilts beneath the pier, supporting it against wind and weather. Voices rose, laughing, from the beach back along the shoreline. The music from the carousel began to play—like the echo of a thousand hand organs reaching across time.

Caro sighed happily, and put her hand through Tony's arm. He smiled and looked down at her. "There aren't many places in the world where you can look out over the ocean and feel the sun shining on your back in January," he said.

Caro nodded. "It's a special place," she told him. "I don't ever want it to change."

Tony nodded. "I know what you mean. That's the way people always feel when things are good." He was silent a moment. "But change comes, Caro," he went on. "Sometimes it makes us happy and sometimes it doesn't, but it happens just the same. That's the way life is."

"That doesn't mean I have to like it," she said.

"No, you don't. But you'll be a lot happier if you make the best of it. You might even find out that you like what happens after all. Some changes that don't seem so good in the beginning turn out to be blessings in the end."

"We're talking about the baby, aren't we?"

Tony nodded again. "I'm sorry you're feeling unhappy about it." She never could fool Tony—not about anything.

Caro shrugged. She couldn't tell anyone yet—not even Tony—how she felt because she didn't really know. It was something she didn't want to think about. At least not right now. "I'll get used to the idea," she told him. "I was just surprised. That's all."

He squeezed her arm. "That's my girl," he whispered.

Caro smiled, then looked quickly away, because she felt an unfamiliar burning at the back of her eyes. Things were going to change, all right. Their whole family would be different, and Caro had liked it exactly the way it was.

Tony turned and motioned for Bandit to jump to the ground. "Time to go to work," he said. "See you at five o'clock, honey?"

Caro nodded and watched him go. It was always the same. Tony would walk along the pier, grinding his hand organ while Bandit collected pennies, tipped his little hat, and occasionally did a few fancy tricks. This meant that Caro was free for the rest of the day. She could stay on the pier and watch the fishermen. She could wade along the sandy beach and look for shells. She could visit the shops and talk to the pier people— that's what they called themselves. They seemed like one happy family to Caro, always laughing and joking and watching out for one another.

But there was one thing Caro never failed to do and that was to ride the merry-go-round. Tony always gave her a little money for lunch or a snack, and an extra quarter for a ride. She told him she would rather ride all day and not eat at all, but Tony didn't like that. So she paid for her extra rides out of the salary Flo gave her for helping at Maria's.

Caro started walking along the boardwalk now, wrinkling her nose with pleasure as she passed Sea

View Snacks right next door to the Bait and Tackle Shop. The smell of fish bait mingled with the odors of hot nachos—crisply fried tortilla chips—smothered with melted cheese and chili. She peered through the window and saw Mrs. Olivetti cutting crusty pizza into thick slices. On a plastic tree rack hung soft twisted pretzels, still warm and sparkling with crunchy bits of rock salt. Caro bought one and held it in her fingers, licking at the salt and taking small bites to make it last longer.

The skate rental shop was busy, and dozens of pairs of urethane wheels skimmed over the worn boards of the wooden walkway with soft, whirring sounds. One skater carried a portable radio and wore earphones. A sign on his back said: I carry my music with me. Caro smiled, thinking of the old nursery rhyme about the woman on a white horse at Banbury Cross. *Rings on her fingers and bells on her toes; she shall make music wherever she goes.* There was something nice sounding about that—something that resisted change.

From a few doors away came the *Pop! Pop!* of Ricardo's Target Guns, and beyond that was Mr. Murphy's Shell House. Caro always stopped there to see the shells of all sizes and shapes and colors. She loved to look at them and at Mr. Murphy's collection of stones from the sea. Sometimes he polished them in the small workroom at the back. "You want to be amazed, Caro?" he would ask her. "Just come back here and look at this."

Caro was amazed. Mr. Murphy always found the beauty under the surface of things. "Stones are just like people," he told her. "There is always something special inside."

Madame Zorinna, the fortune-teller, was next door to Mr. Murphy. She had a velvet-covered table inside with a big crystal ball on top. Lots of people came and paid good money to have Madame Zorinna look into it, but Caro knew that it was nothing but a hunk of glass. One day she had overheard Zorinna talking to Tony.

"I can't tell anybody's fortune," she had said, "and I don't know anybody who can. I just listen to people's troubles and try to give them some good, commonsense advice."

Caro thought it was too bad that people didn't know they could go to the Original Maria's and get good, commonsense advice from Flo for the price of a hot tamale.

The thought of hot tamales made her hungry. She stopped at Walt's Hot Dogs on a Stick, bought a corn dog, and covered it with mustard. Walt glared at her, and she knew he thought she was using too much mustard. Walt thought everybody used too much, and he was always threatening to ration it out in tiny plastic packages, one to a customer. But Caro knew he never would. Walt was all bark and no bite.

She grinned at him. "How are you today?" she asked.

"Compared to what?" he growled.

Caro ignored that and bit into her corn dog. "Delicious," she told him.

"Humpgh!" he answered. But she saw one corner of his mouth twitch, and she was satisfied. That was the closest Walt ever came to a smile.

Caro laughed out loud. Nothing bad could happen here, she thought. The pier was a magical, enchanted place, where everything always turned out all right. She ate the last of her corn dog, threw the wrapper into one of the blue trash bins that seemed more like a decoration than a garbage container, and walked over to the ticket window of the carousel. The red booth was painted with sea nymphs, lions' heads, and a golden sunburst.

Caro counted her money and bought three tickets. Then she went inside the big red building, where an ornate, wooden railing encircled the merry-go-round and kept people waiting until the gate was opened at the end of each ride. The ceiling sloped steeply upward from the corners, following the slant of the roof and leaving plenty of room for the top of the carousel. Caro had never been to a circus, but she imagined that the inside of a circus tent would feel something like this.

Caro watched the carousel slow down and come to a stop as she took her place in line. There weren't too many people in front of her. If she was lucky, she would make it on the next ride.

"Hurry! Hurry! Step right up! Choose your charger! Select a steed! Pick a prancer!"

That was Mr. Lindstrom. He spoke with a Swedish accent that made his voice go up and down just like music. Mr. Lindstrom sold the tickets, then opened the entrance gate to let the customers in. After that, he ran around like crazy helping people choose their horses and making sure everybody was buckled up. When he was sure everything was OK, he would wave his hand at Katie, his wife, who sat in the center of the carousel, turned it off and on, and kept an eye on the gears while it was running.

When Mr. Lindstrom finally signaled that it was Caro's turn, she joined the others who raced to pick one of the forty-six, handmade wooden horses. She passed up a chariot, painted ivory and decorated with sprays of pink and blue flowers. Why would anyone want to sit, Caro wondered, when it was possible to soar on horseback?

Caro chose a white horse this time and climbed on. She had worked halfway around the carousel, riding one horse at a time, and she was going to keep it up until she had ridden all forty-six of them. Then she guessed she would have to start over again, because she intended to keep riding the carousel whenever she

34

got a chance for the rest of her life.

The music started, and Caro held on to the brass pole, waiting for the platform to move. Her horse began to rise slowly, then faster. Up and down. Up and down. Around and around she went. Music filled the air, and Caro felt like singing. The center mirrors flashed, catching colors like a blinking kaleidoscope. She held on with one hand and stretched out her other arm when they passed the ring machine. Her finger caught a silver loop and pulled it free. She didn't mind that it wasn't the golden ring. When she had first come here with Angie, she hadn't been able to reach far enough to catch any rings at all.

Caro always wondered why time seemed to pass so quickly when good things were happening. In her mind, she willed the music to go on forever, but she could feel the gentle change in tempo as the carousel finally slowed for the third time. The music stopped with Caro's horse still high in the air. She slid easily down the side and stood for a moment listening. For a second, she thought she heard an echo, and then it was gone.

Her legs felt unsteady as she jumped from the platform, almost as if she had been in a boat on the water. Mr. Lindstrom was already ushering the next customers in, and she knew she had to leave. But she turned for one last look, memorizing the details of the horses and the ornate roof.

There was a balcony that ran all the way around the room, suspended from the wall just above the top of the carousel. It was enclosed, but there were windows in it—large, square ones about two feet apart. Caro had seen them dozens of times. But she had never before seen anyone looking through them.

There was a girl up there, watching her. A girl about her age, with straight black hair and dark eyes. Caro stared at her, but the other girl didn't look away. She

35

didn't make a motion or a sign with her face. She just stood there, as if she belonged.

"Are you riding again?" Mr. Lindstrom asked. Caro shook her head. When she looked up again, no one was there. Whoever it was had disappeared.

Caro made her way outside. She thought she knew everyone on the pier, but she had never seen this girl before. She must have climbed the steps at the side of the building to get up there. Caro had seen the steps, but she had never climbed them because it didn't look as though there was anything very interesting at the top.

Now Caro walked along to the edge of the building and stopped. The girl was there, coming down the steps. She didn't even look embarrassed at being caught. Caro could see that she was Asian. Maybe she was lost. Probably she didn't even speak English.

"What were you doing up there . . . at the top of the stairs?" she asked, taking a chance.

The girl smiled. Her teeth were very perfect and very white. "I live up there," she said, in English that had an accent but was perfectly understandable.

Caro raised both eyebrows. Lived up there? She had to be kidding!

But the girl only laughed. "I really do," she insisted. "My whole family lives on top of the carousel."

5
Thu Anh

The girl smiled again and said, "Come on. I will show you." She led the way up the steep wooden staircase.

Caro hesitated, remembering what Mary Ruth Jefferson had said at school. "All these Asians are ruining the country. My father says so. He doesn't want me to have anything to do with them."

Caro knew what that meant. If you wanted to be Mary Ruth's friend, you'd better not get chummy with the wrong people. If Caro was seen standing around and talking with this girl, Mary Ruth would cut her out without a second thought. She glanced quickly over her shoulder. None of the kids in Mary Ruth's gang were at the pier today. They hardly ever came. Mary Ruth said she had better things to do—like shopping and going to the movies. So if Caro talked to this Asian girl today, who would know the difference?

Caro looked over her shoulder one more time, then quickly ran up the steps. The chance to see a house at the top of a merry-go-round was more than she could resist. At the top of the stairs, the girl turned and asked, "What is your name?"

"Caro. That's short for Carolyn. What's yours?"

"Thu Anh. That isn't short for anything."

They looked at each other. "How do you spell that?" asked Caro.

"That? T-H-A-T. That."

Caro smiled. "I mean your name. How do you spell your name?"

"Just the way it sounds. T-H-U A-N-H."

"That's not the way it sounds to me. When you say it, it sounds like T-O-O A-N-N."

"That's because you're listening in English." Thu Anh turned and opened the door. "Come in, Caro. This is where I live."

Caro stepped into a long hall. There was one closed door on her right and another one straight ahead at the end of the passage. She could hear the music from the carousel playing. The sound came right through the walls. Thu Anh opened the door at the end of the hall, and the music seemed louder. "Would you like to see the balcony?" she asked.

Caro followed her through the doorway and stepped into a long cross corridor that went to the right and to the left. There were windows on the far side, set about two feet apart. This must be where Thu Anh had been standing earlier, watching the carousel. Caro peered through one of the windows. Sure enough—there it was! Spinning like a top beneath them. She could look down and watch the people as they rotated past. She could see the colored lights reflecting in the mirrors. But most of all, she could hear the music, rising like hot air, lifting and soaring to the tip of the sloped roof.

She turned to Thu Anh and smiled. "It's wonderful!"

Thu Anh smiled back. "I think so, too. This balcony goes all the way around the building. I like to walk

38

along and look through the windows and listen to the music."

Caro looked along the corridor. There were doorways at intervals along the wall opposite the windows. "Do you live in the whole thing?" Caro asked.

"Oh, no! These are apartments up here. The balcony goes by each one of them. We are lucky to have the rooms nearest the outside stairs. The other tenants have to walk through the entrance hall, then along this balcony to their apartments."

"The other tenants?"

"Of course. Mr. Murphy lives here. Right next door. Do you know him?"

Did Caro know Mr. Murphy? Good grief! She knew all the pier people. Probably a lot better than Thu Anh did. But she just nodded her head. "I visit his shop sometimes," she said.

Thu Anh smiled and put both hands on her hips the way Mr. Murphy liked to do. "You want to be amazed?" she imitated in a deep voice. "Just come back here and look at this."

Caro stared at her. "You've been in his back room?"

"Sure, but so have you, I'll bet."

Caro nodded. "Who else lives up here?"

"Mrs. Olivetti and the Lindstroms. Then comes Madame Zorinna. She only has one room and a bath. But she has a crystal ball in her living room just like the one in her fortune-telling place. This one has a hole in the bottom, and she can turn it upside down and put flowers in it. Someday I'm going to check the other one and see if it's a flower bowl, too."

Caro grinned. She was beginning to like Thu Anh more and more. Checking out madame's crystal ball was exactly the kind of thing she would do herself.

"Walt lives up here, too," Thu Anh went on. "He has the room between Mr. Murphy's and madame's. He says he doesn't like madame's singing or Mr. Murphy's rock polisher. For two cents he says he would move, but he can't because of the carousel. He's gotten used to it, and the music puts him to sleep at night."

She led the way back through the hallway and unlocked the closed door that Caro had noticed near the entrance. Inside was a little living room that opened into a tiny kitchen. Beyond that were three small bedrooms. In each room there were windows looking out over the ocean and the pier. You couldn't see into the merry-go-round area from here, but you could hear the music. It came through the walls like flour through a sifter, slightly lighter, but just as much of it.

"What's it like," Caro asked, "to hear the music all the time?"

"It only plays until midnight," Thu Anh said. "But when you live with it all the time, you miss it when it stops. Sometimes at night I wake up and hear the silence, and I wish the music could play forever."

"I know what you mean," Caro said softly. "It makes me have an empty feeling when it stops, the same way I feel when dinner is over but I'm still hungry."

Thu Anh was looking at her. "Being hungry is a terrible thing," she said. Her voice was suddenly different. It sounded sad and angry at the same time. "I never want to be hungry again."

Caro realized with a shock that Thu Anh really meant it—and that she sounded as if she knew what she was talking about. Even when Caro had lived with her mother and Angie in the old apartment, she had never been hungry. Not the way Thu Anh meant. There had always been food in the house, even if it wasn't very appetizing.

She wondered . . . "Are you a refugee?" she asked. The words came out before she could stop them. "I mean . . . I just wondered . . ."

"It's OK." Thu Anh smiled at Caro's embarrassment. "I don't mind being a refugee. It means that my family found refuge. We are safe now. We have a place to live and work, and we have found friends. Sometimes—many times—we miss our old home, but we feel lucky. We are the 'Boat People.' Do you know what that means?"

Caro shook her head. She had read in school about people who sometimes spent their whole lives living on boats. They were called "Boat People," too. But she thought Thu Anh was talking about something different.

"It means we escaped by boat. My family and I left Vietnam at night. It was very dangerous. My father had made secret plans, and we joined other families like ours who could no longer live without freedom. We left our homes after dark and met quietly on the beach. There was a boat waiting, but it was too small. When we all got on, there was no place to lie down, only room to sit, side by side, pressed tightly together.

"For ten days there was very little water and even less food. The sea was rough and the sun was hot. Children cried. Many people were sick. Some died. I didn't think we would ever see land again."

Caro saw her shudder, and she felt a chill go down her own spine.

Suddenly Thu Anh shook herself—as if to clear her mind of the past. "But we are here now," she said. "My father is a good sailor, and he brought us to land safely. After a long time in resettlement camps, we came to America. And here we are!"

She spread her arms wide and grinned at Caro. "So what's your story?" she asked.

Caro was startled. In her mind, she was still somewhere on the water, in a crowded boat with Thu Anh and all those other people. She had never before realized what being a refugee really meant. She wondered how Thu Anh could stand to talk about it. Caro didn't like to talk about the bad things in her own life. But listening to Thu Anh made her a little ashamed that she had ever complained at all.

"Well . . . I live on Bundy Street," she began. "We . . . my family, that is, live behind the Deli. Tony's Deli. Tony married my mother, see, and Angie and I moved across the street. Con came, too, because his stepfather beat him all the time. And of course there's Bandit—the monkey."

She took a deep breath. How was she ever going to explain her complicated family so that Thu Anh would understand? But Thu Anh was staring at her. Her eyes were wide and her mouth was open.

"A monkey?" she asked.

"Sure. That's what I'm trying to tell you. Tony runs the Deli, but he's also a hurdy-gurdy man. You know, an organ-grinder. Bandit is his little monkey. He lives with us in our house. Whenever Tony has time to come here to the pier, I come with him. I've never come by myself, but I'd like to. I love it here. I love the carousel. I love the ocean. I love the sea gulls. I love . . ."

"You are full of love," Thu Anh laughed. "And you are the first person I have ever known who lives with a monkey. I think you are very lucky."

"So are you," Caro replied. "You live with the carousel."

"But not all the time," Thu Anh told her. "After school I help my parents at the cafe. You know— Sinbad's, the one at the end of the pier where you go down the steps by the water. My father bought the cafe a few months ago . . . on time payments, of course. My father says it will take a long time, but someday Sinbad's will finally be ours."

"But Sinbad's doesn't have Vietnamese food," Caro protested. "At least it didn't the last time I was there."

"Of course not." Thu Anh laughed. "We eat Vietnamese food at home," she explained. "But at Sinbad's my parents make American breakfasts, good hamburgers, and spectacular BLT's. But my father says he needs to find a sensational recipe for chili." She took Caro by the arm and pointed her toward the door. "Come on and see for yourself. We'll walk out to the end of the pier, and you can meet my family . . . if you want to, that is."

Caro grinned. There was something about Thu Anh that made her feel really good. "I have to meet Tony at five o'clock," she said, "and it's only four now. That gives us plenty of time."

They walked together along the pier to the wooden staircase near the end. When they passed Tony and Bandit, Thu Anh wanted to stop. Caro reached into the pocket of her pants and pulled out half-a-dozen pennies. "Watch!" she said and bent down low, holding out one hand. Bandit saw her and came quickly, letting out a little squeal. He took one penny, then another, tipping his hat and dropping the coins into his pocket.

"Now you try it." Caro took Thu Anh's hand and put the other pennies in it. "Just open your hand and wait. Bandit will do the rest."

Thu Anh looked at her doubtfully. "Will he bite?" she asked.

"Of course not. He has very good manners."

Thu Anh knelt, one knee on the asphalt, held out her hand, and waited. Bandit came close and cocked his head. He looked at Caro, then at her friend. Tony was watching them, smiling. He gave a little tug at Bandit's rope and made soft kissing sounds with his lips. Thu Anh looked at Tony and began to imitate him, making almost the same sounds. Bandit came closer, took the coins from the palm of her hand, and pocketed them. Then he turned a complete somersault.

Caro clapped her hands. "Good for you!" she cried. "He only does that when he likes somebody. Isn't that right, Tony?"

Tony laughed. "That's right. Somersaults are reserved for special persons."

Was Thu Anh a special person? Caro wondered. Mary Ruth sure wouldn't think so. She would take one look at Thu Anh and turn thumbs down. Caro thought that was a little like deciding you weren't going to like a new food without even tasting it. She had only known Thu Anh a little while, but she felt as if they had been waiting to be friends for a long time. All they had needed was a chance to get together.

Thu Anh looked up at her and smiled, and Caro was absolutely sure that Thu Anh felt the same way.

6
Sinbad's

Caro followed Thu Anh down the steep steps to the lower level of the pier. The flooring here was made of wide planks, laid across the supports so that there were spaces between the boards. When Caro looked down, she could see right through to the water, rising and falling below. It was perfectly safe, but it always gave her a funny feeling to walk around down here, almost as if she were standing on a boat and she could feel the water moving beneath her.

The surface wood was worn smooth, and the planks were wet and slippery where water sloshed from buckets of live bait and where freshly caught fish flapped until they lay still. This was a favorite spot for fishermen and it was often crowded, especially near the entrance to the cafe, where men in rubber boots and floppy hats congregated to talk and sip coffee.

But they smiled and stepped aside when they saw

Thu Anh, and Caro followed her easily into Sinbad's. There were three small booths against one wall and a counter with twelve stools against the other. The two stools at the far end were empty, and Thu Anh headed for these.

A man in a large white apron was standing behind the counter with his back to them. He carefully lifted the corner of a pile of shredded potatoes, then slipped his spatula underneath and turned it. There was a sizzling sound, and Caro saw him crack an egg with one hand and drop it onto the grill, while with the other hand he reached out just in time to catch a piece of golden bread as it popped up from the toaster.

"Is that your father?" Caro asked.

Thu Anh nodded. "He won't be able to talk to us now. He is too busy."

Caro could believe that. He moved constantly, without stopping, but with a kind of rhythm that made one movement flow into the other. It was really fun to watch him. Caro wondered how he could remember what to do next without stopping to think about it.

"Why is he cooking breakfast when it's the middle of the afternoon?" she whispered to Thu Anh.

"People eat breakfast here all day." Thu Anh shrugged. "Don't try to understand it. It's just the way things are on the pier."

Caro wished she could accept things that easily. When she saw something she didn't understand, she always wanted to know the reason why. And when she didn't, she kept trying to find out. Sometimes her mother said she drove the whole family crazy asking questions. But Caro couldn't help it. Not knowing the answer to something was like having an itch and not being able to scratch it.

Through an opening in the wall—a kind of pass-through with a broad shelf on the bottom—Caro could see into part of the kitchen. A woman, wearing the

46

same kind of white apron as the man, was moving quickly and gracefully—peeling, washing, chopping, and cleaning up. Suddenly, she looked up, saw Thu Anh, and smiled.

She is very pretty, Caro thought, with dark hair like Thu Anh's, only pulled back tightly out of the way. Her skin looked soft and smooth and was the color of warm sand. But it was her eyes that were so special, shaped like a fawn's, large and dark and lifted slightly at the corners so that she always seemed to be smiling.

When she saw that Thu Anh and Caro were together, she rinsed her hands and dried them, then came out to the counter.

"Mother, this is Caro," Thu Anh said. "We met at the carousel."

The woman held out both hands and took one of Caro's. "Hello, Caro," she said. "I am Mrs. Truong, and I'm very glad to meet you. Do you come often to the carousel?"

Caro smiled. The woman was still holding her hand, but it didn't make her feel uncomfortable. It made her feel welcome. "Whenever I can," she answered. "I come with my stepfather, Tony Genovese."

"Ah . . . the man who brings music with him . . . and has a little monkey. I have heard many good things about Mr. Genovese. He is said to be a man who has never met a stranger."

Caro thought about that. People were always strangers when they first met, weren't they? She remembered how she felt when she saw Thu Anh for the first time. She had even wondered if she should be seen talking with her. She still felt a little uneasy when she thought of Mary Ruth and the gang at school. She wondered if Tony could look at a person and see a friend, even before he knew that person's name. Didn't he ever wonder what other people thought? She stored the questions away in her mind. When she

47

had a chance, she would talk to Tony about them.

"Tony is a wonderful man," she told Mrs. Truong. "Everybody likes him." She knew that was true. Everywhere they went, somebody was always waving at him or calling him by name.

"Are you girls hungry?" Mrs. Truong asked. "Come into the kitchen," she told them, without waiting for an answer.

The kitchen was small. Much smaller than Flo's. But there was a lot going on in there for such a little place. Pots and pans hung from the walls, their bottoms shining as if they'd all been freshly scrubbed. A giant chopping board was heaped with a pile of freshly sliced onions, and stainless steel bowls were overflowing with lettuce and tomatoes and grated potatoes. Caro could smell chili simmering on the stove. It smelled good, but it didn't smell sensational. What Mr. Truong needed, Caro thought, was to come to Bundy Street and visit Chico. Chico made the most sensational chili in the world.

Wire baskets of brown onions and big potatoes were stacked on one counter, and next to them was the largest pile of raw hamburger Caro had ever seen. Mrs. Truong began shaping thick patties with her hands, pressing and slapping until each one was perfect. She stacked them on a platter, putting strips of waxed paper between them. When the platter was heaped high, she put it on the shelf of the passthrough. Almost immediately Mr. Truong's hand appeared and whisked it away.

Caro looked around slowly. There was a single window above the sink. This looked out on the side of the pier where the steps came down so that every time you looked out you would see feet—unless you leaned way over to one side and got a glimpse of ocean. All the walls were lined with counters and cupboards, and everything gleamed with stainless steel and fresh

48

white paint. There was a calendar on the wall by the door, but she couldn't read it because it was in Vietnamese. She wondered if that would be a hard language to learn—there were so many pronunciation marks over the words. Then she wondered if it had been hard for Thu Anh and her family to learn English.

Thu Anh took three red apples from the refrigerator and a box of cookies from a cupboard. "We can sit at the table," she said, "and you can meet my brother, Tien."

Caro realized with a shock that there was a boy in the kitchen. He had been sitting at the little round table in the corner all the time, reading a book. He was so quiet she hadn't even noticed him.

He looked up at her now, but he didn't say a word.

"Hi," Caro said. "You must be Tien."

He nodded. But he still didn't speak. Maybe he hadn't learned English like the rest of them. But that didn't seem logical.

Thu Anh put the food on the table and Tien reached for a cookie. He seemed very serious, Caro thought. Maybe he was just shy. He appeared to be a couple of years younger than Thu Anh—about Syl's age. Caro immediately wished she hadn't thought of Syl. She didn't like remembering the way she had looked, standing alone on the corner. Caro took a bite of her apple and chewed it thoughtfully. She hoped Syl wouldn't still be waiting there when they got back.

"Do you want an apple, Tien?" asked his sister.

He shook his head and took another cookie.

Caro didn't care if he was Thu Anh's brother or not. The kid wasn't very polite. "Cat got your tongue?" she asked, teasingly.

Thu Anh reached out quickly and touched her on the arm. "You must excuse my brother," she said. "He does not speak."

"But he understands English, doesn't he?"

"Oh, yes. He can read it and write it very well. Tien

49

is a good student at school."

Caro nodded. He was probably just having a hard time with his pronunciation. She could understand that. But he needed to practice or he would never learn how to say the words.

Mrs. Truong began to hum softly while she worked. The melody was sweet, rising and falling gently, like the ocean waves at low tide. Tien lifted his head, listening. His eyes looked far away. For a second Caro thought she saw his mouth move, but he made no sound. When the song was over, he took another cookie and went back to his book. Caro saw the title. He was reading *Huckleberry Finn* by Mark Twain. Tien Truong might not have much to say, but he was no dummy.

There was a cuckoo clock hanging on the wall over the doorway. It made a buzzing sound, and then the door opened to let the bird come out. It sang its message five times and disappeared.

"Five o'clock!" exclaimed Caro. "I have to meet Tony at five o'clock." She got up quickly. "It was nice to have met you, Mrs. Truong."

Thu Anh's mother turned and smiled. "Don't worry, Caro. Our little bird is ten minutes fast. You will make it on time."

"I'll walk up the stairs with you," said Thu Anh, "and then I must come back here and help. Five o'clock is a busy time for us."

Outside, there was a chill in the air, and the sky was already turning golden in the west. "Winter days are too short," Caro said. "I'll be glad when summer comes and it stays light longer. It's wonderful at the beach on summer evenings."

"But that's a long time off," Thu Anh reminded her. "Are you going to wait until summer to come back to the pier?"

Caro hesitated. She felt as if she were about to step

over an invisible line—the kind of line Mary Ruth liked to draw. She took a deep breath. "How about next Saturday? If Tony is busy, maybe I can get permission to come alone."

"I'll be here," Thu Anh promised.

Caro turned to go, then changed her mind. "Maybe we can help your brother with his pronunciation. I wouldn't mind. It would be kind of fun."

Thu Anh shook her head. "Thank you, Caro, for offering, but it is not his pronunciation that needs help."

"But I thought . . ."

"My brother has not spoken for a long time. Not since we traveled on the water. When we lived in our old home, he used to chatter until sometimes my mother would tell him to be quiet for just a moment. But on the water he was so afraid. Three times the pirates came. They took our food and clothing and money and left us with nothing. When they saw that there was nothing left to steal, they took some of our people to sell as slaves. Tien became very quiet. And then he just stopped talking. He has not spoken since that time."

"Not a word?"

Thu Anh shook her head. "There is nothing the matter with his voice. The doctors all say that he is able to speak . . . and yet he cannot. I have seen him try. I have watched him stand in front of a mirror and try to make sounds. But nothing comes out."

Caro didn't know what to say. She hated herself for making that dumb crack about the cat getting his tongue. "Do you think he will ever get better?"

"Perhaps. But it is very hard for him here on the pier. I don't think my mother and father know it, and Tien doesn't want them to find out. But I have seen the look on his face, and I know that my brother is terribly afraid of being near the water."

7
The Girl Who Wouldn't Go Home

Caro thought about Tien all the way home on the bus. She wondered what she would feel like if she wanted to say something, but no words would come out. If she had to keep all her thinking bottled up in her head Caro knew she would explode pretty soon.

Did Tien feel that way, too? Did he still try to make sounds when no one was looking? Or had he given up, so that he just listened and watched . . . and didn't even try to whisper?

Whispering made her think of Syl. Sappy Syl, who didn't talk just because she had decided not to.

Little creep, she thought.

Thinking about Syl was enough to ruin a perfectly nice day. So Caro concentrated on remembering the pier and the carousel and Thu Anh. It had really been a great day!

It kept on being great until the bus rolled up to

Sixty-third Street and stopped. Wouldn't you know it? There was Sappy Syl, standing on Chico's corner, waiting.

Tony saw her and said something under his breath. He looked angry, and Caro didn't often see him that way. "It's dark," he said. "That child lives twelve blocks from here. What is her mother thinking of, letting a ten-year-old child wander around on city streets at night?"

Caro didn't know Syl lived that far away. But if she knew her way to Bundy Street, she sure ought to know her way home. She started to say that Syl was perfectly safe. Who on earth would want to bother her? If anybody tried to kidnap a kid like that, they deserved just what they got.

But a look at Tony's face stopped her. "We'll take her over to the Deli with us," he said, "and then I'll walk home with her."

That was exactly what Syl wanted, Caro thought. She was always angling for extra attention. When Caro got off the bus, she tried to glare at Syl hard to show her how she felt. But Syl was looking at Tony. Her eyes were big, and she held onto the lamppost with both hands. He took one look at her, pushed the organ cart with Bandit inside it toward Caro, and scooped Syl up without a word. He put his arms around her and held her tight.

"It's OK, honey," he said. "I'm going to take you home now."

The things that happened next Caro played over and over again in her mind for days, like scenes from a movie that she didn't quite understand. The whole thing would make sense if only she could fit all the parts together. But there was always something missing, like the lost piece of a jigsaw puzzle.

First, Syl began shaking her head no, as if she would rather stand on that dark corner all night than go home. Not a sound came out of her mouth, but Caro could see the shape of the word on her lips.

"What's the matter, Syl?" Tony asked. His voice was so gentle, it made Caro shiver. Syl hung on to him with her arms around his neck and her legs around his middle. Her head kept going back and forth like one of those carnival dolls with a hinged neck. Once it started, it couldn't seem to stop.

She mouthed some words again, and then her throat made a kind of catching sound, like a cough. Only she wasn't coughing. Syl was crying. She was shaking her head and crying all at the same time.

Caro didn't know what to do. She was standing there feeling helpless when the door of Chico's Cabin opened, and Chico looked out. "Anything wrong, Tony?" he asked.

Caro stared at him. Of course something was wrong! Why did grown-ups always ask questions like that? Careful questions, as if they were afraid they might be intruding?

"Thanks, Chico," Tony said. "I think I can handle it."

"OK. But you know where to find me."

Chico looked at Syl a minute. There was a sad expression on his face. When he glanced at Caro, Chico didn't seem to see her. And when he closed the door, he shut it quietly. Chico was usually a real door banger.

The streetlamps flickered and went on just as the lights from Chico's went out. Tony motioned for Caro to bring the organ cart, then went to stand at the corner, waiting for the traffic light to change. Syl had stopped crying. Her head was on Tony's shoulder, and he was patting her back. Caro could see her face. As she watched, Syl slipped her thumb into her mouth and closed her eyes.

Still sucking her thumb, Caro thought, and she must

54

be ten years old. How disgusting! She looked away quickly. Seeing Syl like this gave Caro a feeling she didn't understand. A disturbing feeling. It was the same way she had felt earlier that day when they were all at Flo's and Caro was scrubbing some of Syl's dirt off. She had reminded Caro then of a puppy nobody wanted, and it had made a lump come into Caro's throat.

Caro looked away from Syl and focused instead on the yellow neon lights above the doors of the Universal Mission. They were directly under the large, gold-painted figure that looked like George Washington, and they blinked constantly like a big advertisement. PRAYER CHANGES THINGS.

Off—on, Off—on.

Caro wasn't sure whether or not she believed that. Their mother had taught Angie and her a prayer to say at night when they lived in the old house across the street:

> Now I lay me down to sleep,
> I pray the Lord my soul to keep.
> If I should die before I wake,
> I pray the Lord my soul to take.

Caro had said it, but she hadn't liked it. The words made her feel uncomfortable. She didn't want to die before she waked, and she wasn't sure she wanted her soul going anywhere without her. She didn't know about other prayers, but that one hadn't been worth much.

Caro looked at Syl again, with her thumb in her mouth. She felt kind of sorry for her, even if she was a little creep.

Could anything change Syl? Caro wondered. She thought it would be a pretty tall order, even for God.

"Caro . . ."

She jumped when Tony said her name. The light had changed, and Caro followed him across the street, wondering what he intended to do with Syl. Was he going to take her home, even when she said she didn't want to go? If he didn't, he couldn't just keep her. He would have to call her mother, wouldn't he? Did Tony know Syl's mother?

Caro realized with a kind of surprise that Jessica talked about their mother all the time and about their nice house and yard and the private room that she didn't have to share with anyone. But Jessica never invited anybody over. Nobody Caro knew had ever seen Jessica's mother or the house or the yard or Jessica's special room. As a matter of fact, Caro didn't know anything about Jessica Smith's family, except what Jessica had told her.

When they reached the other side, they could see Jessica herself coming along Bundy Street from the direction of the Oak Apartments. She was walking fast, almost running—a shadowy figure in the light of the streetlamps, but there was no doubt that it was Jessica. Caro could tell that walk anywhere—a kind of pigeon-toed twitch that made Jessica's long straw hair swing from side to side. She saw now that Jessica walked with her head high and her nose in the air, even at night.

When Jessica reached the Mayan Theater, she stopped and put one hand over her heart. *Dramatic*, Caro thought. *You're always so dramatic*.

"Is that my little sister, Sylvia?" she asked. "Oh, Mr. Genovese, what a relief! I've been looking all over for her. My mother was just about to call the police."

Syl sat straight up in Tony's arms. Her thumb fell out of her mouth. She looked startled at the sound of Jessica's voice. Caro thought she held on tighter to Tony.

"Come on, Syl. We've got to get home." Jessica reached for her, and Syl pulled away.

56

"Is your mother home right now, Jessica?" Tony asked.

Jessica tucked her long hair behind both ears, which made them stick out at the sides. She kept fiddling with the strands, combing them with her fingers. "Sure, Mr. Genovese. Of course she is. Why do you ask?"

Tony smiled at her. "I just thought she might be out looking for Syl . . . like you are," he said.

Jessica looked flustered. "Well—uh—we thought one of us ought to stay home. . . . You know, in case Syl came back or the telephone rang . . . or something." She tried to smile back, but something went wrong with her mouth. It kept twitching sideways. She closed it tight and tried to look Tony in the eye, but she couldn't. She kept blinking and looking away.

She is lying, Caro thought. She had seen her lie before, and she was lying now. *Look at her, Tony. Can't you tell she's lying?*

Tony could, but he didn't act mad. "Is everything all right, Jessica?" he asked.

Her voice went all high and squeaky. "What could be wrong? Look, my mother has dinner on the table, and I've got to go. Come on, Syl!"

"How about it, Syl?" asked Tony. He smoothed her hair with one hand—or tried to smooth it. It was so dirty it was stiff.

Syl shook her head hard. She leaned close to whisper something in Tony's ear. But the words carried and everybody heard her say, "It's cold at my house."

"Shut up, you!" exclaimed Jessica. "You're always telling lies. You ought to be ashamed. Now come on with me. We've got to go!"

Tony opened the door of the Deli. "Caro," he said, "you just go along inside and take Syl with you. I want to have a word with Jessica . . . privately," he added, as Caro hesitated.

He put Syl down on the sidewalk. She didn't protest, but took Caro's hand and held it hard. Caro didn't know what she was going to do with Syl when they went inside, but she went anyway, and closed the door behind her. The little bell rang, and her mother came out of the back rooms.

"There you are!" she exclaimed. "Just in time for dinner. Did you . . ."

She stopped short, looking at Syl. "Hello there," she said. "I didn't know Caro had company."

"She's not really company," Caro tried to explain. "She's . . . she's . . ."

"Where's Tony?" her mother asked.

"Outside, talking to Jessica." She said the word, *Jessica,* with special emphasis and rolled her eyes at her mother as if to say, *and look what I got stuck with in the meantime.*

Her mother nodded, not sympathetically, but as if she understood something Caro didn't know anything about. "Caro, why don't you and Syl run along to the back of the house? It's warmer there. There's a good program on tv. Angie and Con are watching it."

Her voice was soft and sweet, but there was a tone in it that told Caro not to argue. She led the way to the rooms at the back, with Syl hanging on to her all the way. Caro heard the front door open and close and knew that her mother had gone outside with Tony and Jessica.

"I guess you can sit there." She motioned to a chair. It was soft and comfortable and Caro's favorite. She didn't know why in the world she was offering it to Syl.

The skinny little girl fell into it as if she were exhausted. When Angie turned and raised one eyebrow questioningly, Caro could only shrug her shoulders in reply. She smelled dinner cooking in the oven. Roast chicken, she guessed. That usually meant mashed potatoes, tiny green peas, a wonderful tossed salad,

58

and hot apple pie. Syl sniffed and let out a long sigh. Caro sure hoped they didn't have to have her here for dinner.

The little bell rang again, and she heard the front door close. In a few seconds her mother was in the room with them. She walked to the oven and turned down the heat, then adjusted the burners beneath the vegetables. "We'll eat a little later tonight," she announced. "As soon as Tony gets back."

Caro looked at Syl. Her eyes were closed. She looked as if she were settling in for the night. "Where did Tony go?" Caro asked. "Why didn't he come and get Syl?"

"Tony went home with Jessica," her mother said. She didn't answer the other question.

Con looked up, an expression of alarm on his face. "He went to Jessica's neighborhood at night? They didn't walk there, did they?"

Caro's mother shook her head. "Tony has better sense than that. They took a cab, and Tony will ask the driver to wait. Everyone knows that Jessica's neighborhood is no place to be walking after dark."

That was when Caro began thinking about the things that had happened—about Syl waiting on the corner and not wanting to go home, about Tony being angry because she was there, and about Jessica being so nervous and in such a hurry.

She tried to fit the puzzle together, but there were still too many missing pieces. Finally, the only two things Caro knew for certain were that she was getting very hungry, and that there were a lot of things she didn't understand.

8
Jessica's Tall Tales

When Tony came back, he had Jessica with him. "Here we are!" he called. "I hope dinner's ready because I'm starved."

Jessica didn't say much of anything. Tony suggested that she sit next to Angie at the table, since they had been in school together for years. But still Jessica didn't talk. Caro thought that was really strange, because Jessica usually had a lot to say to Angie—about what she had done over the weekend with her mother or her new clothes or her bedroom that was being redecorated for the thousandth time.

Caro watched her. Jessica's face was pale. She was looking straight ahead, but she didn't seem to be seeing anything. She looked as if she was scared but didn't want anybody to know it.

It was a weird dinner, with everybody being extra polite and nobody eating much except Syl, who stuffed the food into her face as if she hadn't eaten for a month. Caro remembered the huge plate of tamales and enchiladas and tacos and beans that Syl had gulped down at Flo's that very day. How could she be so hungry all the time?

Caro was full of questions. She knew better than to ask them now, but that didn't keep her from wondering. She especially wanted to know if Jessica and Syl were just here for dinner . . . or what?

The meal was finally over, and it was obvious that no one was going to tell her anything except that Jessica and Syl would be staying for the night. Tony said they could sleep with Caro and Angie. The way he said it put a period on the whole subject. *Plunk!* And nobody said another word about it, not even later in the bedroom when all the lights were out.

Angie had loaned Jessica a pair of pajamas, which were too tight, but she had said, "Thanks," and put them on anyway. Not a word about the brand-new silk ones she undoubtedly had or her four-poster bed with carved wood and a canopy cover.

Caro found a pair for Syl that she had outgrown, but when Syl put them on, they were so big that they hung on her like a clown suit. By that time Syl didn't know what she was wearing—or care either. Caro's mother had given her a bath, and Caro figured it had worn her out. She had even washed Syl's hair and dried it with an electric blow dryer. It was still the color of bleached straw, as if somebody had emptied a clorox bottle over her head, but it wasn't stiff anymore.

Caro slept with Angie and gave Jessica and Syl her bed. She was glad to do it. Her only other choice would have been to sleep with Syl.

When she opened her eyes in the morning, the other bed was empty. "Hey, Angie," she said. "They're gone."

But Angie was gone, too. Caro pulled on a pair of

jeans and an old shirt and went looking for somebody who could tell her what was going on. Angie and Con were sitting together at the table in the kitchen. But they weren't eating, just sitting there.

Caro poured herself a glass of orange juice and sat down with them. "I overslept," she said. "Where is everybody?"

Angie buttered a piece of toast and handed it to her. "Mom has gone home with Jessica and Syl to help them pack some things. Tony is over at the flower shop talking to Old Lu."

"Old Lu? What for?"

"She's their aunt, isn't she? Tony says she'll want to know what's happened."

Caro put her juice glass down with a thump. "What *has* happened?"

Angie glanced at Con. He nodded his head as if to tell her it was all right. "Caro is old enough to keep her mouth shut, Angie. Anyway, she deserves to know what's going on."

Angie reached over and touched Caro's hand. "Look, Caro, you've got to promise not to say anything about this to anybody. Jessica and Syl have had enough trouble without kids at school talking behind their backs."

"What kind of trouble?" All Caro had ever heard from Jessica was how great everything was.

Angie took a deep breath and began. "Things never were the way Jessica said. She and Syl didn't live in a nice house with a garden. They didn't have candles on the table or steak on their plates. From what Tony said, they sure didn't have their own bedrooms. They were even more crowded than we were when we lived in the old place."

Caro nodded. "Jessica was lying. I'm not surprised. She lies about lots of things."

Angie shook her head. "I don't think she was lying,

62

Caro, as much as she was pretending—trying to make things seem better than they were."

"What about their wonderful mother who took them to all those fantastic places? I'll bet she made that up, too."

"That's the worst part of all. Their mother had a lot of boyfriends, and they were always coming to the house. When she was . . . entertaining, she didn't want Jessica or Syl around. She locked them out of the house when she wanted privacy.

"That's why Syl was always wandering around. Especially after school on Fridays. Then last month their mother left. Jessica told Tony it was a couple of weeks before Christmas. She didn't leave a note or anything. Just disappeared one day and didn't come back.

"Jessica and Syl have been living there alone. All by themselves, Caro, in that awful part of town! They had a little money that Jess had saved out of what her mother gave her every week for groceries. They used that for food, but it didn't last very long. Their mother hadn't paid the utility bills for a long time, so the gas and water got turned off—and then the electricity. That's when they got really scared. They were alone there at night and it was cold and there weren't any lights."

Caro put her toast down. She didn't feel much like eating anymore. "Didn't anybody know what was going on? Why didn't Jessica tell somebody?"

Con answered her questions, taking the first one first. "I think everybody on Bundy Street suspected something was wrong, but nobody knew exactly what. That's why Tony went home with Jessica last night. He felt that it was time somebody found out.

"Jessica didn't tell anybody because she was ashamed and scared. She thought people would laugh at her if they found out all those stories she told weren't

63

true. And she was afraid the county people would come and put her and Syl in foster homes, and they would never see each other again. Even worse, she told Tony, they might make her and Syl go and live with Old Lu and Took because that's the only family they have now. She told Tony it would be like going to live in a funeral parlor."

Caro guessed Jessica was talking about all the flowers at Old Lu's flower shop. Personally, she thought they smelled good and that Jessica was making a big deal about nothing, as usual. She didn't blame her for not wanting to live in the same house with Took, though.

Angie got up and started clearing the table. Then she seemed to change her mind and sat back down again. "Poor Jessica," she said slowly. "She was trying to take care of things all by herself. I don't think she had a single person she could talk to. She had a way of turning people off with all her boasting and fine manners." She hesitated, then, almost as if she were thinking out loud. "I know I sure never acted like a friend to her. If I had, maybe she would have told me things— and we could have helped her sooner."

Poor Jessica? thought Caro. *What about Syl? She must have been so scared and lonely.* Caro knew what it was to be scared and lonely, and she wouldn't wish that on anybody. Not even on Syl.

Out loud she said, "That's the trouble with adults. They know things are going on, but they don't tell kids about them because they figure we're too young to know. Golly, Angie, I never would have called Syl a creep if I had known her mother . . . well, if I had known she couldn't help being a creep."

Angie put one arm around her. "Maybe the lesson is that we shouldn't ever call anyone names. For any reason."

Caro knew she was right. But that kind of reasoning

64

took away all her excuses and made her feel terrible.

The three of them were still sitting around the table when Tony came back. He poured a cup of coffee and sat down. Caro had been going to ask him if he wanted to go back to La Mirada today. It would have been fun to surprise Thu Anh. But one look at his face told her that he had other things on his mind.

"Jessica and Syl will go and live with Old Lu," he announced. "She still has a spare room, even with the flower shop taking up the front of the house. She didn't know they were having so much trouble. Their mother is her sister, but the two of them haven't spoken for years. As soon as she knew, she agreed to help."

"Jessica isn't going to be very happy about that," said Angie.

Tony raised his eyebrows. "Old Lu is a good person," he said. "She'll take good care of the girls."

"I didn't mean that. I was thinking about Took."

"Oh . . . well, I guess the feeling is mutual. When I was there, Took wasn't exactly a fountain of joy. But Old Lu said she would skin him if he made any trouble, so I think he'll leave Jessica alone."

The bell rang as the front door opened. Caro looked up and saw her mother, followed by Jessica and Syl. Their arms were full of paper sacks, and parts of clothing were spilling over the tops.

"I forgot to tell you," said Tony, "that the girls will be staying with us for the rest of the week. Their Aunt Lu says she has to clean the junk out of the extra room, and then find a couple of beds to put in there." He looked at Jessica. "She would like you to come over and talk to her about working in the shop after school."

Caro thought Jessica brightened perceptibly. Give her a little time, Caro thought, and everyone would be hearing about where she lived, about how much money she made from her job, and about how her aunt loved to take them special places on the weekends.

Jessica, she decided, was a survivor.

But she wasn't so sure about Syl. She just stood there holding her paper bags and waiting for somebody to tell her what to do. Angie started talking to Jessica; Con and Tony went off together. Mother handed Caro her bags and headed for the kitchen. That left the two of them—Caro and Syl.

So much for La Mirada, Caro thought. She looked at Syl. Her pimples were worse today. And she looked dirty again, even after that bath last night. "What am I going to do about you?" she said out loud.

Syl didn't say a word—just stared at her and waited. Caro looked out the front window and saw that it was beginning to rain.

For the rest of the week, Tony had said: Syl and Jessica would be staying at the Deli for the rest of the week, and this was only Sunday morning.

From the other room, Caro could hear the sound of Jessica's voice. It was a little too loud, and she was laughing a little too hard. Everybody had found out the truth about Jessica, Caro thought, but she didn't think one single person knew the real person who was Syl. Could there be someone special inside that bony frame? Something as amazing as the beauty Mr. Murphy uncovered when he polished his stones?

Syl looked up at her then and smiled, showing her broken tooth. There was only one thing Caro could do. "Com'on, Syl," she said. "I'll help you put your things away."

9
Bundy Street Blues

On Monday, it rained harder, and the rain didn't stop for the rest of the week. Every day Caro sloshed to school and back, then went to Flo's in the afternoons. Syl was with her every step of the way.

Flo didn't seem to mind. "Syl does look a lot better than she did," she said to Caro.

"That's because of all those baths Mom's giving her." Caro sighed. "The way she looks really isn't the problem, Flo. It's always having her right *there*. Every single minute. I feel as if I have an extra shadow."

Flo reached out and gave Caro a hug. "Being close to you makes her feel good. I imagine feeling good is a new experience for that little girl. If you ask me, Caro, that's pretty important."

It might be, Caro thought, but that didn't make it any easier to have Syl around all the time. She was cramping Caro's style. Caro was trying to be nice, but she found herself looking forward more and more to junior high next year when she and Syl would go to different schools.

By Thursday, the old newspapers and boxes were cleaned out of Old Lu's spare room. On Friday, she sent word that she had found a couple of beds at a rummage sale.

"Hurray!" Caro said when she found out. And then, because Syl got such a hurt look on her face, "Look, Syl, you'll have a bed of your own now, and you won't have to sleep with Jessica anymore." *Or in the same room with me,* Caro was thinking.

Jessica and Syl moved on Saturday afternoon, carrying their paper bags down the block and across the street in the rain. Caro and Angie went, too. "To help," they said, and "to see the new bedroom" that Jessica was already bragging about. But Caro knew the real reason. She and Angie were going over there with them to make sure they stayed.

"The worst thing I can imagine right now," Caro whispered to Angie, "is to wake up tonight and discover that both of them have sneaked back and are sleeping in our room again."

"Shhh!" warned Angie. "They'll hear you!" But she started to laugh, and Caro knew she had been thinking the same thing.

When they got to Old Lu's, they were amazed. There was a van parked in front with SIGN LANGUAGE written on the side, and two men were putting a big new sign on the front of Old Lu's: FLOWER'S BY MARYLU.

"Who's MaryLu?" Jessica wanted to know.

Took came out the front door and answered. "It's my mother's name, stupid. And that's what everybody's going to call her from now on." He stuck his thumbs in his belt and glared at everyone but Angie. When he saw her, he just said, "Hi, Angie," and looked at her as

68

if he couldn't quite believe she was real.

Old Lu came out and stood with him on the little front porch. They were quite a pair, Caro thought. Took still looked like a weasel, and his voice was whiny. But his nose didn't run all the time, and he was a lot cleaner than he used to be. Old Lu was little and skinny, and her skin was tanned a deep brown and wrinkled like a dried prune. Tony said that came from spending so many years outside at the open-air flower stand that used to be across the street.

For a long time, only a few people on Bundy Street even knew that Took and Old Lu were related. Took pretty much did his own thing, and Old Lu didn't seem to pay much attention to where he went. But after Con's accident, and Took's long illness, Lu moved her flowers into the old abandoned house and turned it into a shop. Took worked there after school every day.

Old Lu opened the door wide. "Come in," she said. Jessica sailed right past her as if she owned the place, but Syl hesitated halfway up the steps, and Caro had to take her by the hand and pull her along the rest of the way.

The smell of fresh flowers filled the house. They were in refrigerated glass cases in the front rooms and stacked in vases on the counters and tables. Caro took a deep breath, but she saw Jessica wrinkle up her nose until they passed the open door of the kitchen where a pot of beans was cooking. They smelled almost as good as Chico's, Caro thought.

It didn't take long to carry the paper bags back to the bedroom and dump the contents in the drawers of an old chest. Caro looked around. The walls were a faded blue color, and the white ceiling was cracked, with long spiderweb designs across the surface. There were no curtains at the window and no spreads on the beds. But Old Lu had put a bouquet of flowers on the chest.

"Look, Syl, aren't these pretty?" Caro asked. Syl put

out one finger and felt the ruffled petals of the pink carnations, then gently touched the fronds of fern that Old Lu had added to the vase.

"Carnations smell wonderful. Go ahead and sniff them," Caro urged. Syl put her nose right up against the flowers and grinned. Then she reached out to touch the petals again.

"Stop that!" snapped Jessica. "You don't know anything about flowers. You're not supposed to touch them, you little creep!"

"Don't you *dare* call her that!" Caro felt such a tightness in her throat that she could hardly speak. But she got the words out and was surprised at the fury of them. "What do you know about flowers?" she demanded. "How can you tell what they feel like if you don't touch them?"

"That's right." Old Lu was standing in the doorway. "Most flowers like to be touched . . . and talked to."

Jessica stared at her as if she were crazy. "You talk to flowers?" she asked.

Old Lu didn't bother to answer. She just went to stir the beans. Syl trailed along behind her, sticking close, as if she wanted to be right there in case Old Lu should find some flowers she wanted to have a conversation with.

Jessica rolled her eyes at the ceiling. "I don't know how I'm going to stand this," she told Angie.

Took heard her. "Have ya got another choice?" he asked.

Jessica glared at him. "How dare you speak to me in that tone of voice? You are nothing but a little . . ." She caught herself before she said anything else. The two cousins just stared at each other.

Caro crossed her fingers tight for luck. Syl was in the kitchen with Old Lu, and Took and Jessica were practically fighting. If she and Angie slipped out now, no one would even know they were gone. She gave Angie a nudge, and they were on their way: out the front door, down the length of Bundy Street, and across to the Deli.

"We made it!" Caro said and went to change the sheets on her bed. Everything was back to normal, she told herself. It would be wonderful not to hear Jessica's voice for a while—or to trip over Syl every time she turned around. Caro wondered if a new baby would be as much of an inconvenience as two extra kids.

While she was stripping the sheets from the bed, a piece of paper fell to the floor. She picked it up. It was a drawing—a kind of rough sketch—done in pencil and shaded carefully. Caro stared at it a minute before she recognized herself. Someone had drawn a picture of her. But who? And how had it gotten in her bed? She studied the sketch carefully before she put it away in a drawer. Then she forgot all about it.

Tomorrow was Sunday, and she was going to talk Tony into going to La Mirada. Thu Anh had been expecting her today, but the rain and the moving had spoiled that. Never mind, Caro thought. Tomorrow the sun would shine. The weatherman had promised. She would take the bus to the beach and ride the carousel and see Thu Anh. Caro was not so worried about what Mary Ruth Jefferson would say; she'd had too much fun with Thu Anh the last time—probably as good a time as she could have at one of Mary Ruth's parties.

Caro was sure nothing would keep her from going to La Mirada on Sunday. But something did. In the morning it was still raining. About one o'clock Syl came back, and a few minutes later Jessica arrived. "She really does talk to flowers," Jessica said. "It's weird . . . really weird over there."

They got out the Monopoly game and everybody played. When they were tired of that, they popped popcorn and looked at tv. When Jessica said, "Well, I

71

guess we should be getting along," nobody argued. Not even Tony.

On Monday, it rained harder. Winter storms came blowing in from the Pacific Ocean, battered the coastline, and followed a windy path inland. By midweek, the gutters of Bundy Street were like rivers, and the intersections by Chico's corner and Old Lu's were lakes. When the traffic went through, the cars made slushing sounds and sprayed dirty water high up onto the sidewalks.

"I'm sick of this," Caro complained to Angie when they were doing the breakfast dishes on Saturday morning. It was exactly two weeks since she and Tony had gone to La Mirada.

"I thought you liked rainy weather. You always said you did."

"That was when I didn't have anything else to do. It's nice to sit by the window and read a book when it rains. But it's been raining for almost two weeks."

"Well, the schools haven't closed. You can always do your homework."

Caro didn't think that was worth answering. She gave Angie what she hoped was a haughty look and went up to the front of the Deli. She took a pickle from the jar and bit into it with a crunch. It was really sour, and she felt her mouth pucker all the way to the back of her head.

She looked out the big window at the front of the store. From here she could see all the way up and down the other side of the street. Smoke was coming from Chico's Cabin, rising in a gray haze and dissolving into the rain. Hoang Chou's Laundry wouldn't open until later, but there were lights in the windows on the upper floor where Hoang Chou lived with his wife, Amy, and eight kids. Next was the old green house where Caro used to live, and beyond that was the Original Maria's, the Second Chance clothing store, and Old Lu's on the corner.

Bundy Street was caught in a wet gray blanket of falling rain that held it fast. Caro put her arms around her waist and hugged herself tight. It was daylight, but it was dark outside—dark and cold—except for the little spots of warm light that came from the windows and flashed from the neon sign next door above the mission: PRAYER CHANGES THINGS. Off—on. Off—on.

Was it really true? Caro wondered. Could you really talk to God? And did he change things? The neon sign flashed again, sending spurts of light into the mist. Caro thought about what Tony had said that day at the beach. *Sometimes change makes you happy and sometimes it doesn't.*

She had a sudden vision of half the people in the world praying for what they wanted and the other half getting stuck with what they never asked for. She was sure that wasn't the way it was supposed to work. She didn't think God handed out favors willy-nilly like that. Then how did he decide which prayers to answer? He must have a system, but she sure didn't know what it was.

Are you listening to me now, God? Caro wondered. *I have a few things I wish you would take care of.* Maybe, she thought, it was important to say please. *Could you please do something about Syl? You know what I mean; let her stand on her own two feet so she doesn't always have to stand on mine. And can you please make her stop being afraid? While you're at it, it would be nice if you could show Tien how to talk again—and make Jessica not talk so much. Also, could you please do something about Took? I know he has improved a lot, but he sure has a long way to go.*

Caro hesitated. Her prayer sounded much like the list she used to write at Christmastime for Santa. She wondered if it sounded that way to God, too. So she added a few thank-yous, like thank you for my new friend Thu Anh. Maybe God liked to be thanked, just as anyone did.

But there was one more problem; she hadn't mentioned it before because it seemed even more selfish. She looked around the Deli to make sure no one had walked in. Then she leaned her head against the cool glass of the window. "I don't want to be cooped up forever," she whispered softly. "Oh, God, I want to walk in the sunshine. I want to ride a white horse and listen to the music play. I want to fly!"

10
Kaleidoscope

Late Saturday night the wind began to blow: a strong
north wind that whistled and roared and filled the air
with so much static electricity that Caro could see the
sparks in the dark when she rubbed her hands across
her blanket. By morning, the clouds were gone, and
the sky was a deep, clear blue. The wind was still
blowing a little, but the sun felt warm. When Caro
looked up and down Bundy Street, she could see that
the gutters were dry, and the pools of water flooding
the intersections were already receding into little pud-
dles.

"Look, Tony!" she cried. "What a perfect day for the
beach." She loved La Mirada after a rain. Even the
sand seemed to have had a bath.

But Tony shook his head. "I can't make it today,
Caro. I'm really sorry."

"Then let me go! Please, Tony. I'm old enough. I've

gone with you lots of times. I know the way there, and I know my way around the pier. Besides, I won't really be by myself. I'll be with Thu Anh the whole time." She took a long breath and let it out slowly. "Oh, Tony. I need to go!"

He looked at her a minute without saying anything. He rubbed his chin slowly. "I can't think of a reason to say no," he told her. "You already walk clear across town to go to school every day. I can't see why you shouldn't take a bus to go somewhere else. Let's see what your mother thinks."

Her mother didn't think it was such a great idea. "It's a long way," she protested. "All sorts of people ride the city buses."

"All sorts of people walk around on Bundy Street, too," Caro reminded her. "And it's not a long way at all. It only takes fifteen minutes, and that's because of the traffic."

"What would you do all day by yourself?"

Caro looked helplessly at Tony. "Tell her," she begged. "No, I'll tell her myself. There's the carousel and Thu Anh and the fishermen and the pier people and the sea gulls and the water and shells on the beach. Look, Mom, how long has it been since you took off your shoes and walked in the soft sand?"

Her mother was giving her a strange look. Suddenly, she smiled. "Too long," she said softly. "I guess I needed to be reminded of what the beach is like at your age. . . ."

"At any age, Evelyn," Tony corrected.

"Yes, I guess you're right." Her mother smiled at Tony, and then looked back at Caro. "But I want you to be home before dark. Be sure to catch the four o'clock bus. And take your sweater in case it gets chilly," she added.

Caro gave her mother a look that said thank you. She noticed that her mother looked obviously pregnant now. Her stomach was swollen beneath the smock tops she wore, but she didn't look as ridiculous as Caro had first imagined. And she wasn't as tired as she had been. In fact, Caro thought, as she grabbed her sweater from the back of a nearby chair and put it on, her mother was almost as much fun as she had always been.

"Flo paid me yesterday," Caro said, knowing that her mother had forgotten one question she might now ask. "I have plenty of money to buy a corn dog and ride the merry-go-round, too. . . . I've gotta go. Good-bye—and thanks!"

Caro edged toward the door, opened it, and went outside. She didn't look back. It had been her experience that looking back always gave somebody a chance to foul up her plans to go forward. She went straight to the corner and crossed to Chico's. The bus would be here any second. She would get on it and the door would close behind her and she would be free. On her own. Without a worry.

"Caarrro," came the wailing cry, all the way down Bundy Street.

It was Syl. She must have come out of Old Lu's and spotted Caro, standing on the corner. Caro saw her start to run—past Second Chance and Maria's. The bus passed her as she reached the old green house. It stopped at the corner, and the door sprang open with a *whoosh*. Caro took hold of the handrail and climbed onto the bottom step.

"Hurry up, if you're coming," urged the driver.

Syl was running as if her life depended on it. Maybe it did, Caro thought. Maybe Syl's life depended on a lot of things besides food and a place to sleep. Caro looked over her shoulder and saw Syl race past Hoang Chou's and skid to a stop at Chico's corner.

"Take me!" she called. "Take me with you, Caro!"

The bus gave a roar. "Make up your mind, sister,"

the driver ordered. "Off or on. It's your choice."

"Syl, I can't take you," Caro called. "Old Lu won't know where you've gone. She'll be worried about you. Go home, Syl. Go on home."

Somehow she knew Syl wouldn't. She would stand there on the corner waiting. Caro remembered how lonely she had looked the last time, and she knew she couldn't stand coming home and finding her that way again. "Never mind," she told the bus driver. "I guess I made a mistake." But she thought, *I made a mistake all right. I should have left five minutes sooner.*

Caro jumped back down to the sidewalk and watched the bus drive away. Then she stood there a few minutes longer. Finally she looked at Syl. "If you want to come with me," she told her, "you'll have to get permission first."

Syl just looked at her, and it occurred to Caro that she probably didn't know what permission meant. "Oh, come on," she said. "I'll get it for you. But hurry up. The next bus leaves in fifteen minutes. I don't intend to miss that one."

Old Lu wasn't home, and Jessica and Took were fighting again. Caro interrupted just long enough to say, "Syl wants to go to the beach with me."

"Take her, and welcome," Jessica snapped. "I'm sure I don't mind."

"What about Old . . . I mean, MaryLu?"

"She won't mind either. You can take my word for it."

"Ha!" Took gave a loud snort. "You can't take her word for anything!"

Caro took Syl and left. There was nothing to do but talk to Tony. Luckily he was in the front part of the Deli, cleaning the cases. "Sounds like a nice idea to me," he said.

Caro raised her eyebrows at him, and he grinned. "It still sounds like a nice idea, Caro. Don't worry

78

about Old Lu. I'll tell her I gave Syl permission."

So that was that. The next thing Caro knew she was climbing on the bus with Syl sitting in the backseat beside her, wondering if she had enough money for both of them to eat lunch and ride the carousel. She thought about Thu Anh. What would she think of Syl? How would Caro and Thu Anh have a good time with Syl along? Maybe, she decided, it would be better if she didn't see Thu Anh at all today. Syl was somebody she would rather not have to explain.

It was midmorning when they got off at Third Street and started down the hill. "Breathe deep," Caro told Syl. Syl did. "Do you smell that?"

Syl nodded.

"Good. Now breathe deep again. The sea air is good for you."

All at once the carousel began to play. The music seemed to lift and soar on the salty breeze, reaching across the sand and up the hill, welcoming them with open arms. "There's the pier," Caro said, pointing. "It's full of fishermen and shops and . . . well, you'll see. The music is coming from the carousel. It's a merry-go-round. Have you ever ridden on one?"

Syl shook her head. Her face was very serious, and her eyes were bigger than Caro had ever seen them. Impulsively, Caro reached down and took her by the hand. "The pier isn't a scary place, Syl. It's fun. You're going to have a good time today."

Syl looked up at her doubtfully. *Well*, thought Caro, *why shouldn't she be doubtful? Her life hasn't exactly been full of good times so far*.

The two girls climbed the cement steps to the top of the pier together and stood looking at the brightly painted booths that stretched along one side and the fishermen that lined the other. Roller skaters whizzed by, their broad urethane wheels humming. The target guns went *Pop! Pop!* Balloons in pastel clusters were floating high, tied securely at the bottoms, but swaying as if they were free. The sounds of happy voices filled the air, and laughter mingled with the music of the carousel. Caro looked around, but she didn't see Thu Anh anywhere. She sighed. It was probably just as well.

"Com'on," said Caro. "It's time for a ride." She bought two tickets and pulled Syl inside the red building with her and into the line. She held tight to Syl's hand because she looked as if she was getting ready to bolt and run. The music stopped, and Caro moved forward—through the gate and onto the turntable, pulling Syl behind her. She glanced up at the glassed-in balcony, but Thu Anh wasn't there.

"Choose a horse, Syl," she said. "Any one you want." Syl looked horrified and didn't move. "OK, I'll choose one for you. How about this blue one? Put your foot in the stirrup and climb on." She gave Syl a boost, strapped her in, and climbed on the one next to hers, on the outside. Syl had turned white, with a greenish tinge around her mouth. Caro hoped she wasn't going to throw up. Some people seemed to have trouble having a good time.

The music started, and the carousel began to turn. The horses were moving, faster and faster, up and down. "Isn't it wonderful!" Caro cried. "Listen to the music, Syl!"

Syl was holding tightly to the brass pole with both hands. Caro realized for the first time that Syl's arms were so skinny that her elbows poked out like bony knobs. She didn't have a sweater, and there were goose bumps all over her skin. But she was listening to the music. Her head was moving back and forth in time with the rhythm. Suddenly she turned toward Caro and smiled. It was a real smile, not Syl's usual pitiful little grin. This smile was full of joy and . . . happiness. Caro couldn't figure out why it made her want to cry.

She blinked hard and smiled back at Syl, and it was then that she saw their reflections in the panels of long, polished mirrors in the center of the carousel. Two bright figures, whirling by like pieces of a kaleidoscope. The colored lights flashed and flashed again, making constantly changing patterns on the glass.

That was the way life was, thought Caro. Constantly changing. And she and Syl were part of the pattern. Some peoples' paths crossed, she decided, and their lives got all mixed up together, just like the little colored pieces in a kaleidoscope. She watched the mirrors as they echoed the shifting lights, and she listened to the rhythm of the music. Each part of the carousel was important, she thought. Each piece of glass affected the whole pattern. Was it possible that the way one single person acted could affect the whole world?

That was something to think about. But not now. The music was slowing, and it was time to get off. If they were going to eat lunch on the pier, there wasn't enough money for another ride.

"Let's go," she said, leading the way outside. They were halfway along the pier, in front of Mr. Murphy's Shell House when Caro saw Thu Anh. "Hey!" She forgot about Syl and waved her arm excitedly. "Thu Anh! It's me—Caro!"

Thu Anh looked at her and smiled and started walking quickly toward them. "Caro! I was hoping you would come today." Then she looked at Syl, and she smiled at her, too. "Hello," she said. "My name's Thu Anh."

Syl just stared at her. She didn't move. She didn't even whisper.

She would introduce her, Caro decided, as her neighbor. Thu Anh would get the point if Caro made a little face. She would understand that Syl was someone that Caro was stuck with for the day.

But Syl reached up and took her hand, and Caro could feel her trembling. She thought of the way Syl had looked on the carousel, when a real smile had illuminated her face. And the words didn't come out at all the way Caro had planned.

"Thu Anh," she said. "This is Syl. She's one of my friends from Bundy Street."

11
Sand Castles

"Which way are you going?" Thu Anh asked.

"The same way you are," Caro told her, "whichever way that is."

They looked at each other and laughed. Syl didn't pay any attention to them. She was watching the woman in the Candy Shoppe swirl a long paper cone through a vat of spinning sugar, collecting the strands like webs of colored silk until the whole thing became a thick pink mass, dotted with darker pink sparkles. Caro jiggled the coins in her pocket. If they didn't eat much for lunch, they could buy one cone of cotton candy.

"Wait a minute," she said to the others. She walked up to the window and put some coins on the counter. The woman started to hand her the cone she had just made, but when she saw that there were three of them, she dipped it back into the vat and swirled it around until it grew to twice that size.

"Oh, that's wonderful," Caro cried. "Thank you!"

She held it out toward Thu Anh and Syl. Thu Anh pulled off a piece and ate it with her fingers, but Syl didn't move. "Go ahead," Caro told her. "It's delicious. It melts in your mouth."

Syl picked off a tiny piece and tasted it. She looked surprised and reached for another. The three of them walked slowly back along the pier toward the carousel, not talking because their mouths were full of the sweet, sticky stuff.

Tony said cotton candy tasted like sugared cobwebs, but Caro didn't agree. This was one of the few times Tony was wrong. She thought it tasted like spun sugar, which was exactly what it was—sugar spun as smooth as soft silk, light and feathery as a cloud. It was almost gone when they reached the steps that led to the rooms above the carousel.

"Tien is up here," Thu Anh said. "Shall we save the rest for him?"

Caro nodded. That was the way Thu Anh was—always thinking of the other person. Caro wished she knew more people like her.

Thu Anh opened the door at the top of the stairs and led the way inside just as the carousel began to play again. "Look, Syl, you can walk along the balcony and watch." Caro led her to the end of the little hallway and through the door to the balcony where they could look through the windows and watch the horses and the colored lights.

"You can hear the music just as well in here." Thu Anh laughed and opened the door to her apartment. Syl followed her. Her eyes were wide with amazement. "You see, Syl, my family lives above the merry-go-round. We can hear the music all day and into the night—until it finally stops at midnight. And you know what? When it stops, we miss it, and we are happy when it starts in the morning again."

Tien was sitting at the kitchen table, drawing on a piece of paper. He looked up once, nodded his head at Caro, and went back to his drawing. "This is Syl," Thu Anh told him. "She's one of Caro's friends." He looked up again and studied Syl curiously. Syl went straight to the table, sat down across from him, and returned the stare. They sat like that for several seconds, looking at each other, until Tien shrugged and went back to his drawing. He had pastel pencils, Caro saw, and he was sketching flowers, using some in a vase in the center of the table as his models.

Syl moved her chair closer and watched him intently. After a few more seconds, she reached out for a piece of paper, stopped when Tien looked up and frowned, and then took the piece anyway, along with several pencils. He rolled his eyes at Thu Anh, before he went back to work, shrugging again as if to say that none of it—or them—mattered.

"Come on, you can help me. That is, if you want to. I'm going to make egg rolls today. Have you ever tasted the Vietnamese kind?" Thu Anh wrapped herself in a huge white apron and handed one just like it to Caro.

Caro put it on. "I don't think I've ever eaten any Vietnamese food."

"Good. Then you're in for a treat." She glanced at the table where both Tien and Syl were working busily. "They look happy," she said. "We can have the rest of the kitchen to ourselves. I'll make plenty of food. There will be enough for all of us for lunch and for my family for dinner, too."

"*Oh, my darling—oh, my darling—oh, my darling Clementine . . .*" The music came up from below and filled the warm kitchen with melody and rhythm. Caro felt a shiver of joy go right down her spine. She was going to eat lunch on top of the carousel! She felt like pinching herself to see if she was really awake.

Thu Anh took some ground pork from the refrigerator and put it on the sink. Then she put some dried mushrooms and something she called bean thread in a bowl and poured cold water over the top. "Here," she said. "You can chop the onion—very fine, if you please—and also the crab meat and a little fresh shrimp." Thu Anh produced those ingredients and handed them over to Caro. She crushed some garlic and chopped a jicama until it looked like fresh, peeled apple bits, then drained the water from the bowl and cut up the mushrooms and bean thread.

"Now we mix it all together," she said. Caro watched her as she added a couple of eggs, a little sugar and salt, and a dash of soy sauce. "This is the fun part," she told Caro. "You can watch me, and then try it yourself."

Thu Anh opened a package of egg roll skins and put some of the filling on each one. Then she folded one up like a long, oblong envelope, wetting the final lap with egg white and sealing it with her fingers. It looked so easy, Caro thought. But when she tried it, all the filling came out in a pile on the sink. Thu Anh laughed. "Try again, Caro. You can do it."

"It's harder than it looks," Caro said. But she tried again—and again. The fifth time, the package stuck together, and Thu Anh clapped her hands.

"Perfect!" she exclaimed.

Caro shook her head. "I'm better with tamales."

"What are . . . tamales?"

"Why they're . . . impossible to explain. I'll have to bring you some." It wasn't hard, Caro thought, to come from different cultures and still be good friends. All you had to do was share your ideas.

She watched as Thu Anh filled the bottom of an electric wok with oil, heated it, and dropped the egg rolls in. They fried slowly, turning golden brown and filling the kitchen with a wonderful smell. She saw Syl turn in her chair and heard her sniff loudly. Tien looked up, rolled his eyes again, and went back to his picture. But Thu Anh said something to him in Vietnamese, and he reluctantly put down his pencil, stacked the papers, and got some plates and little bowls from the cupboard.

Thu Anh put eight egg rolls on a platter in the middle of the table, added a jar of something she called fish sauce, a plate of lettuce, and a bowl of mint leaves. "We eat them like this," she said as she picked up a large leaf of lettuce and lined it with mint. She put a hot egg roll in the middle and wrapped the lettuce around it. Then she poured fish sauce into a bowl and used it for a dip, eating the egg roll in her fingers.

Caro followed her example. "Ummm!" she exclaimed. "Delicious!" The sauce was sweet and sour and a little hot, and it had little shreds of red pepper and carrot floating in it. She grabbed for a napkin as it leaked down her chin. Maybe, she thought, if people all over the world would just cook together, they would stop fighting. It was hard to be angry with anyone when you were enjoying their food.

"Let's see what you've been doing," Thu Anh said, reaching for Tien's paper. She showed it to Caro. It was a nice drawing, but Caro thought it a little stiff. Flowers shouldn't be lined up like soldiers. They should be soft and flexible, ready to blow in the wind. They should look like . . . the ones Syl had drawn.

Caro drew in her breath quickly. Had Syl really drawn these? They were so real Caro could almost smell them. Syl grinned and handed Caro another piece of paper. It was a sketch of Tien—a caricature, really—and he must not have known Syl was doing it or he would have stopped her. The boy in the picture was scowling. His lower lip was poked out. And sitting in the middle of his piece of paper was a large frog with flowers in its mouth. Caro couldn't help smiling. So Syl was the one who had drawn the picture of her and left it in her bed. *Amazing*, Caro thought. *Syl really has talent. She is special. You just have to know her well enough to see it.* Caro passed the paper to Thu Anh, but she had hardly had a chance to glance at it when Tien's hand reached out and snatched it away.

Everyone was very quiet. Tien looked at the sketch a long time. Then he looked at Syl. He was scowling more than ever, and his eyes looked angry. Suddenly Syl stood up and scowled back at him. She pulled her brows down over her eyes and pursed out her lips in imitation, then gave an elaborate shrug. Tien got up slowly from his chair. He took a piece of paper and wrote something on it in Vietnamese and handed it to his sister. Thu Anh looked at it and nodded. "He's going down to the beach for a while," she told Caro.

When he got to the door, he stopped and turned around, motioning at Syl with one hand. She got up and followed him. There was a big smile on her face, and her broken tooth showed. She stood facing him, hands on her hips, and kept smiling, holding the expression so long Caro thought her face would crack. Tien glared at her until, almost imperceptibly, his shoulders began to shake, and his mouth to twitch. He was laughing. His mouth opened to show perfect white teeth. But not a sound came out.

Syl turned to Caro, raised her eyebrows once, as if to say "Look what I'm stuck with!" and followed him out the door.

When Caro and Thu Anh got to the beach a few minutes later, Syl and Tien were already drawing pictures in the damp sand. The tide was out, and there were smooth pebbles and small shells along the edge of the surf. Piles of brown seaweed lay in tumbled heaps.

"I know what we can do," said Caro. "We can build a sand castle. We have all afternoon so it can be a huge one, with a moat and turrets and pieces of seaweed for flags, and we can decorate it with shells and line the walls with pebbles and . . ."

They were all staring at her. Good grief! Was it possible that they didn't know how? She stared back at them. They were all outsiders—each and every one of them! What was she doing here with these characters, anyway? She could imagine what Mary Ruth Jefferson would say if she could see Caro now. Suddenly, Caro began to laugh. She didn't care what Mary Ruth said. Mary Ruth wasn't any fun at all—not the way Thu Anh and . . . yes, even Syl was. Syl had a sense of humor, and Caro hadn't even known it until today. It was a funny thing, she thought, that some of the kids that people didn't want were the ones really worth knowing. If they were going to be outsiders, then she guessed she was, too.

"Look," she said, "we'll start right here—far enough back so the water won't get it and far enough down so the sand is good and wet." She sank onto her knees and began, scooping damp sand up by the handfuls and watching the baby crabs scatter. "We'll build the outer wall first, using the sand from the moat. Then we'll tackle the towers. Well, come on! What are you waiting for?"

The others started, slowly at first, watching to see what Caro was doing. It wasn't long before they got the idea. The castle grew. A magnificent one, Caro thought. And they finished the moat just in time to catch the water that crept closer and closer with the incoming tide.

"It's like a lake," Syl whispered, putting seaweed leaves carefully on the surface to float like little boats.

Suddenly a larger wave rose and broke, sending foamy water rushing toward shore. Tien jumped far back out of the way, but Syl stood with both arms outstretched. "No! No!" she shouted, then clapped her hands over her mouth. The water poured into the moat, filled it, and capsized the outer walls. The tallest tower fell, dissolving into a soft pile of slush.

"Oh, Caro, it's ruined," said Thu Anh. "All that work and it's ruined!" To Caro's surprise, Thu Anh stamped her foot. "That's not fair," she said.

Caro started to laugh. So Thu Anh could get mad at things and lose her temper. Caro realized how glad she was that her friend wasn't perfect after all. She looked at Tien. He was scowling and shaking his head at the ocean, putting all the blame there, she supposed. But it was Syl who came over close and looked up at her and whispered softly, "What can we do, Caro? What can we do about it?"

Caro took Syl by the shoulders and looked right into her eyes. It was the first time she had noticed how remarkable they were—a deep lavender blue that seemed to look right through you.

"There's only one thing to do when your castles get knocked down, Syl. You start building all over again. That's the way it is with sand castles—and come to think of it, that's the way it is with life."

Syl looked up at her a moment, then turned and squatted in the sand. She motioned for Tien to come and help her. Then she began digging. Thu Anh looked at Caro and smiled. "Let's help them," she said.

It was like that for a whole month of weekends. The weatherman kept predicting storms, and the northern coast was battered by heavy rains and high tides, but at La Mirada the sun shone, the sand was warm, and the sea was blue, with little whitecaps that turned to frothy bubbles along the shoreline.

Caro and Syl took the bus every Saturday afternoon after Caro had worked at Flo's, and every Sunday, whether Tony came or not.

One Saturday in the middle of March when Old Lu

took Syl and Jessica shopping for the day, Caro went to La Mirada by herself and stayed all night with Thu Anh. They walked along the beach together and collected shells and smooth stones. They watched from the pier as the setting sun turned the sky to crimson and then to gold. For dinner, they ate Vietnamese egg rolls from the Truong's kitchen and hot tamales fresh from Flo's. Finally they lay in bed and listened to the music as it mingled with the sounds of the sea. It was beautiful, Caro thought. It was so beautiful.

The next Saturday, Thu Anh and Tien came inland to Bundy Street. By this time, the morning-glory vines had grown tall and begun to bloom, and there were blue blossoms from one end of the street to the other.

People by the dozens were coming just to see the flowers, and yesterday a large picture had appeared in the newspaper with the heading: Bundy Street Blossoms—Old Neighborhood Gets a Second Chance. Flo thought that was wonderful advertising for her Second Chance clothing store.

"Oh, Caro, it's really beautiful," said Thu Anh when she got off the bus. "It doesn't seem like downtown at all. If you had some artists here, I think it would be like Greenwich Village. That's a place in New York. I've never been there, but I've read all about it. It's an old part of town that came back to life and has lots of trees and flowers . . . and artists."

"Well, we have Syl and Tien," Caro said. "They're artists. I guess that's a start." Caro remembered how ashamed of Bundy Street she and Angie had once been. Now, a friend was complimenting her on the place, comparing it to somewhere in New York City. Well, Bundy Street had changed after Con's accident, and it was a change for the better. Maybe Tony was right: some changes were blessings.

Caro and Syl took Thu Anh and Tien up and down the street, introducing them to their friends. When they got to Old Lu's, Took was there, but because his mother was there, too, he didn't have much to say. At Maria's, Flo invited everybody in for hot tamales, just as Caro knew she would. Amy Chou was busy with her kids, so she waved from the upstairs window. But when they went to Chico's, he didn't even turn around. Caro had known Chico all her life, but sometimes she couldn't figure him out.

When Thu Anh and Tien got on the bus to go back to La Mirada, it was late afternoon. Caro waved until the bus was out of sight, then went to the corner and waited for the light to change. Syl was with her, as usual, but Caro really didn't mind anymore.

"Where'd ya find your little gook friends?" The voice came from behind her, but she could recognize it anywhere. The only person in the whole world who sounded like that was Arnold Tooker.

She whirled to face him. She was so angry she could hardly speak. "Look who's calling who names," she snapped.

"You heard me . . . gook! gook! gook! Those people are over here taking all the jobs away from good Americans."

Caro took a deep breath and spoke as slowly and clearly as she could, walking toward Took all the time. "What would you possibly know about that, *Arnold*?" He began to back away, but she kept right on coming. "If you didn't work for your mother in her shop, you wouldn't be out looking for a job, *Arnold*. You'd be sitting home complaining. You're a whiner and a complainer, and you're also a coward. That's a lot worse than anything you can call my friends."

"Yeah," whispered Syl from behind her.

"So don't let me hear you talk about people who work because they want to. And don't you ever let me hear you use that awful word again."

"Yeah," whispered Syl. She came out from behind

Caro and advanced on Took. "And I'm gonna tell Aunt Lu what you said."

"What's the matter with you guys? Nobody can take a joke around here." Took shuffled away, his hands in his pockets.

Chico stuck his head out the door and said, "That's telling him, kid."

Caro glared at him. "You weren't any too friendly yourself today."

"Yeah," whispered Syl.

Chico shrugged and disappeared inside. "Come on," said Caro, and she and Syl went into Chico's Cabin together. "So what was the matter?" she demanded.

Chico shrugged again and began wiping his counter tops. "I don't think much of all these foreigners they're letting into the country," he muttered. "They're just cluttering up the place."

"Well, I guess you should know, Chico. You came from Puerto Rico twenty years ago. But you didn't even have legal entry papers, isn't that right?"

Chico looked embarrassed. "That was different, kid. I wasn't a refugee."

"I know," said Caro softly. "You were one of the lucky ones."

He waved his wet rag at her. "Go on! Get outta here. You're cluttering up my establishment!"

"I thought," said Caro haughtily, "that I was giving it a little class."

"Yeah," whispered Syl softly.

12
High Tide

Caro did a lot of thinking after that. She could understand Took calling names, because Took was a name caller. But Chico? Of all people, Chico should have understood what it was like to come to a new country. Chico, with his thick, bushy hair that he tied back with a piece of string, and his heavy features that made him look a little scary. He should know that you ought to like people for the way they are, not for the way they look. Caro had known Chico all her life. In spite of the way he looked, he was a real softie. But he wasn't acting kindhearted now.

What about you? Don't you remember how you used to feel about Syl? How you called her a creep and ran away from her on Fridays? a voice inside Caro asked.

She remembered all right. And she wasn't proud of it. *That was before I understood her,* she told herself. *I never called her a creep after I got to know her.* It wasn't much of an excuse, but it was all she had.

Anyway, Syl had changed. She wasn't nearly as bad to be around as she used to be. Except for one thing that really bugged Caro a lot.

"Look, Syl, I really wish you would talk out loud," Caro told her. "You can end up tall or short and it won't have a thing to do with your voice. Honest. You can take my word for it."

Syl looked at her doubtfully. "I don't want to take a chance," she whispered.

Caro groaned. "Well, it's hard on the rest of us, trying to hear you. And you're a bad influence on Tien. Did you ever think of that?"

Syl shook her head. "No I'm not. I am not," she whispered.

Caro had to give up. Syl was right, and everybody knew it. She was a good influence on Tien. She could get him to smile, and sometimes he even stood with her and let the waves come up on the sand and trickle over his toes. That was a real achievement, Thu Anh said, because the closest he ever came to touching water was when he took a bath.

"When we were on the boat," she told Caro, "the sharks came. Every day they came. Hungry sharks. As hungry as we were. Tien . . . he was very frightened. Even more frightened than I. Whenever he looks at the ocean, I think he remembers the sharks. It is a miracle that he will stand now and let the waves wash over his feet."

It was the last Saturday in March when the weatherman began issuing storm warnings again. "Worst storm of the season. Heavy rains, strong winds, and high tides. Waves may reach heights of fifteen to twenty feet."

"They've been forecasting that all winter," Caro protested when her mother had doubts about her going to the beach that day. "Look outside. The sun is shining. It's beautiful. I don't know where the storm is, but it's sure not around here."

"I'd feel better if Tony were going with you," her mother said. "But he can't today. Listen, Caro, a twenty-foot wave would wash right over the top of that pier and take you with it."

Caro laughed and put her arm around her mother. "Will you quit worrying? If there are waves like that, I won't be on the pier. I'll be on the bus, coming home."

Her mother looked at her a minute, then gave a little sigh. "OK, Caro, I'll let you go today, but on one condition. If the weather changes—and it can do it suddenly this time of year—you and Syl cut your day short and head for home." She shook her head. "La Mirada Pier is one of the old ones. The pilings are made of wood instead of concrete. I'm not sure they will weather a bad storm."

"But, mom, the carousel is way back from the water, over the sand. It'll be all right, won't it?"

"I don't know. If they have twenty-foot waves down there, the carousel won't be over sand for long. The water could wash right in under the pier all the way to the base of the hill."

"Then what about the people who live there? The Truongs and the Lindstroms and Mrs. Ollivetti and Madame Zorina and . . ."

Caro's mother groaned and held her hand on her head. "We haven't got room for all your pier people, Caro. Now wait, don't look at me like that. What do you want me to do? Put the entire pier population to bed on our living room floor?"

"There are other spare rooms on Bundy Street," Caro said. "Two apartments across the street are empty. Chico keeps a cot in his back room. I've seen it. I'll bet Flo would think of something. And there's always the mission."

Caro's mother began to laugh. "I hope you grow up

and become a social worker," she said. "Or at least something that lets you take care of people." She reached out and gave her a hug. "Go on," she said, still laughing. "Get out of here. It will probably be a lovely day."

Syl was waiting on the corner, holding a large bag under her arm that rattled when she moved it. She looked up suspiciously at the sky. "See," she whispered, pointing at a long finger of gray cloud that stretched across the horizon.

"Don't worry," Caro told her. "The wind will blow it away." There was enough wind to do it, she thought, zipping up her jacket and pulling the hood over her head. Even Syl had decided to bring a short coat, and she put it on now. It was funny, Caro thought, how chilly the wind could feel when the sun was shining so brightly.

By the time they got to La Mirada, the gray cloud had grown and covered half the sky. And the wind was still blowing. "Give it time," Caro told Syl. "I'll bet it will blow all the clouds inland to the mountains, and we'll have a perfect, sunny day here."

But Caro was wrong. It got colder and darker, and the wind seemed to be bringing more clouds instead of blowing them away. There were thousands of whitecaps on the water, and the waves were large, swelling and rolling toward the shore, then splashing white foam high onto the beach. Still it didn't rain. Caro and Syl stayed on the pier and rode the carousel twice. Mr. Lindstrom let them ride the third time free. He said they were his best customers. As far as Caro could see, they were about his only customers that Saturday.

Thu Anh and Tien were nowhere in sight, which meant they must be waiting at Sinbad's. Caro and Syl walked to the end of the pier, hugging their jackets close about them. Caro thought of the warm kitchen behind the counter and walked a little faster.

Mrs. Truong always let them have the table while she worked at the sink. Sometimes Caro and Thu Anh put together a jigsaw puzzle while Syl and Tien drew with Tien's pastel pencils. Sometimes they all played dominoes or began a long game of Monopoly that they would have to finish the next week. Then they would go back on the beach and work on their latest sand castle until it was time for Caro and Syl to catch the bus home.

But this was not the kind of day to build castles in the sand, and Caro would be glad to feel the warmth of Mrs. Truong's kitchen.

"Hello!" Thu Anh called when she saw them enter the restaurant. "We were not sure you would be able to come today. The weatherman has predicted a terrible storm."

"I know," Caro told her, "but I don't believe him." She looked out the window at the waves that seemed to almost touch the lower level of the pier. The old wooden piles creaked and groaned with the force of the water. "At least I didn't believe him until I got here," she admitted. "If the weather turns bad, we'll have to catch the bus and head for home."

She hesitated a minute before she spoke again. Her mother sure hadn't issued an invitation, but she hadn't exactly said a definite no, either. "You can spend the night at our house if you're worried about the storm."

There, she'd said it and she was glad. She would worry about the consequences later. She was doubly glad when she saw the pleased look on Mrs. Truong's face.

"Why thank you, Caro. Thank you very much. That's very thoughtful of you. I think we'll be all right though. We may have to close Sinbad's early tonight, but the Carousel Apartments are over the sand and should be safe."

Caro felt the floor shudder as another wave swelled and surged forward beneath it. She hoped Mrs. Truong was right. Caro glanced at the clock on the wall. It was only three o'clock, but it was getting darker all the time.

Syl walked over to the table where Tien was drawing and pulled a flat, square box out of her sack. Then she reached in again and took out a plastic bag full of colored marbles. In the square box was a board with little round holes in it. Syl carefully began arranging the marbles in the holes, keeping each color in its own triangular area.

"Chinese checkers," she whispered to Tien. He looked delighted and immediately put his papers away.

Syl turned to Caro. "I borrowed it from Jess," she confided.

"Eeegh! That took a lot of nerve. Did you ask her first?"

Syl shook her head.

"Then you'd better get it back before she misses it. Whatever you do, don't forget it when we get ready to leave."

They all played the game for a while, sitting around the table. But it was hard to concentrate with the wind making so much noise and the waves crashing against the boat dock outside. Caro looked up once and saw that the cafe was empty. She went to the door and looked out. All the fishermen had given up and gone home. The boats were moored against the dock, but they were bouncing around and bumping into each other a lot. Still there was no rain.

Mr. Truong came to the door and stood beside Caro. The dark water of the ocean was covered with white foam. The sea was boiling, Caro thought. Churning and boiling, like a volcano ready to erupt. The little bird from the cuckoo clock sang four times, and Mr.

Truong said, "I think we should go."

They put on their coats and turned out the lights, then stood close together on the deck and waited while he locked the door. Caro saw with growing alarm how close the water was now. She was actually walking in it. The foam came right up and leaked through the open spaces between the wooden planks of the flooring. When the waves surged forward, the deck lifted and fell, and the supports beneath shifted from side to side. It was a dizzying feeling, and she felt Syl grab her arm and hold it for support.

Tien's mother had her arm around him and was pushing him toward the steep steps that led up to the main level of the pier. His eyes were large, and he looked frightened. Thu Anh followed them up, then Caro and Syl. Mr. Truong came last. He turned once to look back at Sinbad's, and Caro thought he seemed worried.

The harbor master's office was still open, but all the shops on the pier were either closed or closing. Wooden shutters covered the windows of all the stores and even larger shutters, which looked like garage doors, were being pulled down over the fronts of the game booths and around all sides of the bumper car ride. It was like a ghost town, except for the carousel. Caro could still hear the music playing. Mr. Lindstrom was a real optimist if he thought he was going to get any more customers tonight. And then she didn't think about any of it anymore, for the wind blew so hard it almost lifted her off her feet, and she had to concentrate on keeping her balance.

She looked over the railing once and was astonished to see how far the water had come. When the waves hit the beach, they crashed like thunder, then made hissing sounds like rushing air as they raced up the slope, reaching their foamy fingers farther and farther along the sand. Suddenly, the rain began. Caro saw it on the macadam before she felt it: big, flat drops that looked as black and shiny as ink—spaced far apart, then closer and closer until there was a steady downpour that drenched them before they could reach the carousel.

"Come up! Quickly!" urged Thu Anh's mother. "You can't make it to the four-fifteen bus on time. I will give you dry clothes, and then my husband will take a big umbrella and wait with you until the four-thirty bus arrives. It's so dark outside. I don't want you walking around by yourselves."

Once they reached the apartment, Mrs. Truong produced a pair of Thu Anh's jeans and a warm sweater for Caro and some clothes that Tien had outgrown for Syl. None of the things fit just right, but it didn't matter. They were warm and dry. Then she heated a pan of milk and poured powdered chocolate into it. They drank it while they looked out the window.

"Are you sure you'll be OK here?" Caro asked. The carousel sat on stilts high above the sand, but the water was moving, and moving fast.

Mrs. Truong smiled. "Don't worry, Caro. I would not want to spend the night out on the end of the pier, but I'm sure it is quite safe here."

She opened a closet door and took out a huge umbrella. "If this doesn't keep you dry," she laughed, "nothing will." She handed it to Mr. Truong. He buttoned up his coat and looked around.

"Where is the little girl?" he asked.

"Syl . . . Syl!" Caro called her name, then called again, louder. "She must be right here. She was drinking her chocolate a second ago."

Thu Anh touched her on the arm. "I saw her, too. She whispered something to Tien, and she seemed excited, but I didn't pay any attention. I know! They must have gone to the balcony to look at the horses—or to talk to Mr. Murphy next door."

Thu Anh's mother and father both ran along the

corridor to the balcony. Caro could hear them calling, "Tien. Syl. Where are you?" Then she could hear them knocking on Mr. Murphy's door.

"Oh, no!" Thu Anh exclaimed. "The Chinese checkers that Syl borrowed from her sister. The game was on the table when we left Sinbad's. I'm sure she didn't bring it back with her."

Whatever you do, Caro had told her, *don't forget it when we get ready to leave*. Jessica would eat her alive if she did, and Syl knew it. But would Syl try to go all the way out on the pier in this storm to get it? Yes, Caro decided. That's exactly what Syl would do—because she thought she had to. And Tien must have thought he had to help her.

Caro didn't stop to think any further, but raced to the outside door, opened it, and ran down the steps as fast as she could. She looked across the sand at the ocean once and then didn't look at it again. The water was too frightening—black and deep and angry— spurting waves high above the iron railings on either side of her as she ran, head down into the wind toward the far end of the pier.

"Caro, wait! I'm coming with you!" It was Thu Anh's voice right behind her. But Caro didn't stop. What if Syl or Tien fell in? What if she didn't get there in time?

The harbor master's office was dark and empty looking. She wouldn't get any help from there. But as Caro started down the steep stairs, the streetlamps that lined the pier went on and cast a misty light across the churning surface of the water. "Syl! Tien! Can you hear me?"

Nobody could hear her. The ocean was making too much noise, and the wind was blowing her words away. She reached the bottom of the steps and felt Thu Anh's hand on her arm—clutching her fingers—holding tight.

"They must be here!" Caro cried.

The water sloshed over her feet. Cold water. Rough water. It sucked at her shoes. Caro held Thu Anh's hand tighter. The water surged as a great wave hit the side of the deck. It was then that Caro realized that the music had stopped. The only sounds she could hear now were the sounds of the wind and the water.

13
"Oh, My Darling Clementine"

The roaring, pounding sound made Caro want to cover her ears with her hands. But she couldn't. She was too busy holding onto Thu Anh with one hand and to the bottom of the stair railing with the other. The wave rushed across the deck, knocking them off balance, sending cold, swirling water up over the tops of their feet and filling their sneakers until they felt sloshy and heavy.

The deck steadied and the water drained away, but in the light from the lamps above Caro could see the next wave coming. It looked like an inky black mountain rising from the sea and hurtling toward them.

Thu Anh pulled at her arm. "We must go back, Caro," she shouted. "Quickly! Up the stairs!"

Just then, a light flickered inside Sinbad's and went out. It could be the electricity, Caro thought, going off and on, or it could be . . .

"No!" She shook her head. "I have to see if they're in there." She ducked her head and held on tight as the wave smashed broadside against the deck and sent a river of water racing over the top. Caro tried not to think about how deep it was—over her feet and half-way to her knees. The waves sucked greedily at her legs with an unpleasant hissing sound.

"Oh, Caro . . . I'm so scared!" Thu Anh's voice sounded high and thin as the wind caught it and lifted it away.

Caro didn't try to answer her. She was scared, too, but she didn't see what good it did to talk about it.

"Come on!" she yelled. Still holding Thu Anh's hand, she splashed and stumbled her way around the side of the building to the door of Sinbad's. Someone had unlocked it, for the knob turned easily in her hand. But when she pushed it open, the wind sent it crashing back against the inside wall. It was all Caro and Thu Anh could do to force the door shut again.

"Syl! Tien! Where are you?" Caro couldn't hear any answer, but a light flashed. Off—on. Off—on. It was coming from the kitchen in back. "There they are!" Caro yelled. "Com'on, Thu Anh. Let's get them out of there!"

A tremendous wave hit the end of the pier and sent a violent shudder through the floorboards of the cafe. Both Caro and Thu Anh fell sideways against the counter, and pots, pans, dishes, and glasses flew from the cupboards and crashed against the walls.

Caro got up and started for the kitchen, but it was an uphill climb. Something had happened to the building. The floor of the cafe was sloping back crazily toward the outside deck, and walking on it was like scaling a mountain. Thu Anh was still lying on the floor where she had fallen. She wasn't even trying to get up.

"Come on! Come on!" Caro urged. But when she leaned over to help Thu Anh, Caro saw that one arm was twisted behind her, bent in a direction that no arm was supposed to go. Thu Anh moaned softly and opened her eyes.

"Go on," she said. "I'll be all right in a minute."

Caro stared at Thu Anh's arm. *Not in a minute, you won't. Not in a month of minutes.* Then she saw the water coming in under the door. There was a big crack at the bottom, and it was running in just like somebody had turned on a faucet. It must be deep out there now. They wouldn't be able to get out that way. She looked frantically around the room, searching for another exit.

The light flashed again in the kitchen. On—off. On—off. Like the sign above the mission, Caro thought. But there were no neon letters spelling, PRAYER CHANGES THINGS. Only that pitiful little light flickering in the darkness, trying to show her where to go.

Listen, God, can you hear me? Are you listening? Caro waited. She looked down at Thu Anh. Her head was on her good arm, and her eyes were closed. *I'm in a lot of trouble here and I could do with some help. Thu Anh is hurt . . . but I guess you can see that for yourself. I'm sure Tien and Syl are in the kitchen with a flashlight. But Tien is scared of the water, and Syl is scared of almost everything. What am I going to do, God? I—I'm not feeling so good myself right now.* She swallowed painfully, not knowing what she was going to say next until the thought came out of her head and seemed to form all by itself.

"Please!" she said out loud. "Please help me. Please show me what to do."

Nobody answered. She didn't hear a sound except the pounding of the ocean and the roaring of the wind. But the light went on again, blinking rapidly, on and off . . . on and off. Suddenly Tien appeared in the doorway. He was holding a flashlight, and Syl was standing close behind him.

106

His hand was shaking so hard that the flashlight beam seemed to dance. Caro looked at the two of them skeptically. *I had a little more help than this in mind, Lord. But if it's all you can manage . . .*

She tried to think, but it wasn't easy. Her head was beginning to throb, and there was a tight, burning feeling behind her eyes. Another large wave hit the pier. There was a terrible sound of wood splintering. Caro felt a whimper begin deep in her throat and clamped her mouth shut tight to hold it there.

You won't be any good if you go to pieces, Caro Rafferty. So just pull yourself together and use your head.

She tried to make her voice sound businesslike when she spoke—as if she were used to being trapped in a waterlogged cafe in the middle of the ocean every day of the week. But she could feel her voice tremble just the same. "Well, Tien, finding that flashlight was a smart thing to do. Why don't you just hand it to Syl while you help me move your sister?"

Tien took two steps backward and would have disappeared out of sight if Syl hadn't grabbed the flashlight out of his hands and shoved him in Caro's direction.

Keep him busy. Don't give him a chance to think. "Be careful now. Her arm is hurt, and I think she may have hit her head. Let's get her up on her knees first, and then we'll see if she can walk. You take one side and I'll take the other."

Caro shook Thu Anh's good arm. "Wake up!" she ordered.

Thu Anh raised her head and blinked rapidly. Caro gave Tien a nod. "OK, Tien . . . NOW!" Thu Anh was on her knees, then on her feet, but she wasn't happy about it.

"You're hurting me!" she said angrily, glaring at her brother.

"Be quiet," Caro told her. "He's trying to save your life."

Tien looked at Caro in amazement. "Well, aren't you?" Caro demanded.

He nodded solemnly. She supposed he had never thought of himself like that. Only as someone who couldn't talk and was afraid of the water.

They helped Thu Anh to a chair where she could rest her head on the table. The Chinese checkers game was lying there beside her, right where Syl had left it. The table seemed to rise and fall with the movement of the floor. Caro thought this must be what it would be like to be on a sinking boat in a rough sea. She held onto the counter and looked slowly around the room. What now?

The only way out of the kitchen was through the little window over the sink. If they could manage to climb out that way, they could crawl directly onto the stairs that were only a few feet away. She pulled a chair over to the sink and climbed up on top, standing with her feet in the basin. The window opened easily: it was the sliding kind that only opened on one side. Once Caro pushed it all the way open, the wind rushed in with a force that almost took her off her feet. Salty water stung her face and arms, but she stuck her head out anyway and tried to see.

The water had risen over the deck and up as far as the bottom rungs of the ladder. She thought it must be waist-deep out there—and much deeper when the waves came rolling through. They had to get out now—or they might not get out at all! As she watched, Caro felt the whole building tremble. It lifted high, like a surfboard on the crest of a wave, then settled suddenly with a lurch.

All at once, the fishing deck in front of Sinbad's collapsed, pulling the bottom half of the stairway with it. There was a ripping, tearing sound as it broke away.

Caro saw the boards separate and fall into the water like toothpicks being emptied out of a box.

Only the top of the stairs was left, and those steps dangled and swayed in the wind, their splintered edges hanging just above the kitchen window. Could they still climb out that way? If they fell, they would drop right into the ocean. Should they even try? As Caro stared out the window, trying to decide what to do, the lights on the pier above blinked once and then went out.

Someone was crying behind her. She turned around and saw that it was Thu Anh. She had raised her head from the table and was looking wildly around the room. Her features were twisted as she sobbed loudly. "We're going to die!" she wailed. "We're all going to drown!"

Syl stared at her, and her lips began to tremble. She reached out and grabbed the Chinese checkers and held the box tightly against her chest. Caro wondered if she were more afraid of the storm or of Jessica's anger when she found her game missing.

Tien seemed confused, as if Thu Anh, by acting frightened, had taken his place, and he didn't know what role to play anymore. He stumbled to the sink and looked up at Caro, waiting.

What now, God? Everybody is falling apart but me, and I don't know what to do.

The wind wailed and howled and water sloshed through the window. Experimentally, Caro held onto the window ledge with one hand and reached out with the other, trying to grasp the edge of the broken stairs. She touched the wood, grasped a solid piece and held on. But the ocean rolled and she almost lost her balance and fell. When she pulled her head back inside the kitchen, she was trembling all over. She might be able to make it. But what about Tien and Syl? And what about Thu Anh? She wouldn't have a chance.

She looked down at Tien. He had taken the flashlight back from Syl and was holding it in one hand, flicking the switch nervously. Off—on, off—on. *If prayer changes things, God, I wish you would hurry. I'm praying, but I feel like screaming. I feel like yelling for help!*

Then do it. Yell for help.

She looked at Thu Anh, with her head on the table and her shoulders shaking, and at Syl and Tien, who were standing together now, watching her. Caro groaned. *Can't you see that I'm the only one who has a voice?*

Then use it. Say something.

But what? What could she possibly say that would make anything better? Thu Anh looked up from the table. "We're dying!" she moaned. "We're all going to end up in the ocean!"

She was giving up, Caro thought angrily. It was wrong to give up. What was it that Flo had told her once? *Not trying is the only way you can really be a failure.*

"Stop that!" Caro shouted. "We're not going to give up. We're going to . . . yell for help. Somebody's out there looking for us. We're going to yell for help until it comes!"

She motioned to Tien and Syl. "Climb up here on the sink next to me—and bring that flashlight with you. Don't just stand there. Hurry up!"

At first they didn't move, but when Sinbad's gave a lurch that sent the kitchen table sliding across the floor, not only Syl and Tien, but also Thu Anh stumbled to the sink and climbed up. Thu Anh did a lot of moaning, but she made it. "Good girl!" Caro said, putting her arm around her.

"Now look, we have to have a plan." *What is it, Lord. What's our plan?* The flashlight felt heavy in her hand. She flicked the switch, and a warm beam of light flared out like a signal . . . a signal . . . "This will be our signal," she told them. "Whoever is out there looking for us will see it—and they will know where we are."

She held it up to the window and began working the switch. Off—on, off—on. *Prayer changes things*. Did it really? Or did it change people so that they could change things?

A remarkable thought went through Caro's mind. Was it possible that God needed people? *Do you, God? Do you need me? Do you need us all to help each other?* A warmness went through Caro that blocked off the cold and steadied the trembling in her fingers. She knew now exactly what she was going to do. She was going to stay calm because that was the way to keep the others calm. And she was going to yell as loudly as she could. No, that wasn't quite right. In a storm like this, they were all going to have to yell together.

"Thu Anh," she said, "your arm is broken, but there's nothing the matter with your lungs. Syl, you can talk, and you can yell, too. You do it every time you think I'm going to take the bus without you." She looked at Tien. "There isn't anything the matter with your voice, either," she told him. "You decided not to talk, but that doesn't mean you can't. I think you're just out of practice. It would help a lot if you could yell with us . . . but that's up to you."

She handed him the flashlight. "You know how to work this." And then to the others, "When I count to three, we're going to shout together. Just one word. *Help*."

They crouched together against the windowsill and watched the flashlight beam filter through the wind and rain and send a misty light toward the top of the pier. Off—on, off—on, it flashed, like a message in the night. "One, two, three . . ." Caro counted. The first shout was pretty wobbly, but they got better after that.

They put their faces to the window and strained their voices. HELP! HELP! HELP!

Tien watched them. Caro saw him. His mouth was forming the words—but silently, without a sound. Still he worked the flashlight switch, holding it as far out the window as he could. If only Tien could shout with them, Caro thought. She was afraid their voices were being carried away on the wind. They needed more strength. They needed Tien.

A gigantic wave struck the pier with such force that they had to hold onto each other to keep from falling. Caro saw with horror that water was covering the floor of the kitchen—getting deeper—swirling and bubbling like a miniature angry sea.

Tien saw it, too. He crouched farther back against the wall above the sink. He looked at it as if it were an animal about to attack. Caro watched him helplessly as he raised his arm and hurled the flashlight at the floor, where it sank into the dark water and disappeared in a pool of hazy light.

"Tien!" she shouted. She was so angry she didn't try to stop her words. "That does it. I told you that you had a choice. But you don't anymore. You can just open your mouth and yell with the rest of us!"

She turned to the window. "One, two, three . . ." she counted. "Well, what's the matter with everybody? I want to hear . . . I want to hear . . . some music! *Oh, God, thank you. Music is the way.*

"Oh, my darling, Oh, my darling, Oh, my darling Clementine . . ." She sang the words, softly at first, then louder and louder. Syl sang with her, and Thu Anh joined in, but Tien sat quietly with his head down and his arms pulled tightly against his sides.

"Come on, Tien. You can do it. I know you can. We need you." For a second, Caro saw the same flicker of amazement on Tien's face that she had seen when he realized he was trying to save his sister.

Let him try, Lord. Please show him how. I think that if he fails now, he's going to have a hard time living with himself for the rest of his life. Don't you see what I mean? This may be his last chance!

Impulsively, Caro reached out and took Tien by the hand. "I'll sing with you," she told him. "Com'on now." They started again, lifting their voices against the wind, sending the music out into the night. Tien's lips were moving. Caro squeezed his hand. He was trying. She was sure of it, but the words couldn't seem to come. Maybe . . . of course! He could read English, and he could understand it, but he had never spoken it. He didn't know how to form the sounds.

She leaned over, shouting against the wind. "You can sing without talking," she told him. "It's really easy. All you have to do is open your mouth and go, la—la—la."

"La la-la la . . . la la-la la . . . la la-laaa la-la la-la," Caro sang.

Very faintly, like a brand-new instrument being tuned for the first time, came the sound of Tien's voice. It wasn't exactly on key, but that didn't matter, for it got stronger and stronger.

And then they were all singing together. Anyone who heard them, Caro thought, would never know they were scared to death, for they sounded exactly as if they were singing for joy.

When she saw the lights coming, then growing stronger, and finally flashing above them on the pier, she felt happy, but she didn't feel surprised. And when Tony was lowered down in a kind of rope harness and dangled outside the kitchen window, it seemed the most natural thing in the world to climb out one by one and hang onto him tightly while someone from the pier above pulled them up.

There were voices, then. Dozens of them. Shouting and crying. Caro felt herself wrapped in a warm blan-

113

ket and held tightly in Tony's arms. She was aware of drinking something hot. She knew she was terribly tired and suddenly sleepy. But the one thing she would never forget for the rest of her life was the sound of Tien's voice, still singing, even after they were rescued.

"La la-la la . . . la la-la la . . . la la-laaa la-la la-la."

As tired as she was, Caro managed to whipser, "Thank you, God. Thank you very much."

14
Save the Pier!

Almost all the pier people ended up on Bundy Street that night. Tony and Chico insisted. They said the pier wasn't safe—not even the Carousel Apartments. And they were right. The whole end of the pier was gone by morning—Sinbad's and the harbor master's and the Bait and Tackle Shop. Mrs. Olivetti's Sea View Snacks hung out over the water, threatening to fall in. The rest of the shops that had been boarded up were OK, but they couldn't open until repairs were made on the wooden piles that supported the pier.

The Carousel Apartments had a lot of broken windows, but those could be fixed. And the merry-go-round wasn't damaged at all.

When Caro woke up in the morning, everything that had happened seemed like a dream. "What were you doing on the pier, Tony?" she asked. "How did you know that we were in trouble?"

He rumpled her hair, the way he always did when he was happy. "Fathers know when their children are in trouble, Caro."

He had never called himself her father before. Caro liked the way the words sounded. Funny he would say that now, so close to the time when his own baby was to be born. Maybe the baby wouldn't make any difference, after all. Tony's words made Caro feel that, no matter what happened, Tony would be on her side.

"When you didn't come home on time," he continued, "I took the bus to La Mirada, and Chico came with me. He and Mr. Truong are the ones who pulled us up by the rope to the top of the pier."

Chico and Thu Anh's father, working together? Caro sat up straight in bed, then groaned when she discovered how sore her muscles were. "I almost forgot!" she exclaimed. "Where's Thu Anh? How is her arm?"

Thu Anh had had to spend the night in the hospital, but she would be home that afternoon. He went on to give Caro a full account of the whereabouts of all the pier people. The Truongs were going to stay at the Deli that day and the next. Mr. Murphy had spent the night at Chico's on his cot in the back room. Walt and the Lindstroms were next door in the mission.

Once Caro knew that everyone was safe, the one joy of last night's experience returned to her mind. "Oh, Tony! Tien can talk. At least he will be able to. Last night he was singing."

"We all heard him. Once he got started, he didn't want to stop. We heard all of you, as a matter of fact. We had already searched the pier, and we couldn't find you. But when we went back a second time, you were singing that song—the one from the carousel. The melody seemed to rise right above the wind."

Tony stopped and cleared his throat, and he waited a few seconds before he tried to speak again. "Caro, it was like a miracle, all of you singing together like that, without any fear in your voices."

"I think it was Tien's voice that did the trick," Caro said. "I told him we needed him."

Tony shook his head. "No, Caro. You needed each other. Not one person all alone, but everyone working together. That's the kind of thing that makes music."

Later that day Caro went to Old Lu's. Madame Zorinna was staying there. She had carried both her crystal balls all the way with her and insisted on putting them on a table in Old Lu's house. Old Lu said it was all right, but Caro saw that they had both been turned upside down and filled with flowers.

Syl was talking a blue streak. Caro listened in amazement. She thought Syl might even be able to outtalk Jessica. She probably already had, for Jess wasn't saying a word about her missing Chinese checkers.

"I hope you're going to run down pretty soon," Caro said. "If you keep that talking up, you'll never grow any taller."

Syl stared at her in alarm. Then, very slowly, she began to smile. She had a nice smile, Caro thought. Even with her broken tooth showing. "That's ridiculous," Syl said. "I'm going to end up short or tall, and talking won't have a thing to do with it. So I've decided to talk."

They went out the door together and headed for Maria's. As they left, Caro saw Syl give a little toss of her head in Jessica's direction. Syl, she decided, was going to be all right.

Mrs. Olivetti was sitting at one of Flo's tables eating hot tamales. "Delicious," she was saying. "I've never tasted anything like them."

"I'll be glad to show you how to make them," said Flo. That's the kind of person she was, thought Caro. She didn't hide her candle under a bushel, and she wasn't selfish with it, either.

Caro walked with Syl to Chico's. They turned around at the corner and looked along the length of Bundy Street. The rain had damaged the morning glories, but they would come back. In a couple of weeks it would look like a country village again.

Mr. Truong was coming out of Chico's. "I can't believe it," he was saying. "I was using all the wrong ingredients. Your chili is the best I've ever tasted. How can I thank you for showing me the right way?"

"My pleasure," Chico said. "You're a fast learner. I'll be glad to have you working here for me until your place is repaired." He cleared his throat uncomfortably when he saw Caro.

When Mr. Truong was gone, Caro and Syl went inside. "What do you think about all these foreigners cluttering up the place?" Caro asked.

"Yeah," said Syl.

"You have a big mouth for a little kid," Chico answered. "Both of you do." He came around to the front of the counter. He was starting to grow a beard and looked scarier than ever. He bent way down and looked Caro in the eye. "You're cluttering up my place again," he told her.

Caro grinned happily. "Com'on, Chico. You know I'm just giving it some class."

Thu Anh came home from the hospital later that afternoon, but her arm hurt, and she didn't feel like talking much. The next day, most of the pier people went home. "We are anxious to find out if the city will repair the pier," said Mr. Truong. "It will be very expensive, and some of us will surely be in financial trouble if the city doesn't help."

"But they have to fix the pier!" Caro cried. "It's important! It's a special place! It's . . ."

"It's expensive," Tony told her. "A lot of people enjoy it, but they may not be willing to pay to repair it."

118

And Tony was right. The newspapers quoted lots of people who thought the pier should be closed down entirely. "What a pity," said Caro's mother. "It's really a landmark—one of the last great carnival piers. But it's more than that. It's a way of life for a lot of people who live there, and it brings pleasure to lots of others. I really think it's the only place in the world where you can live on top of a merry-go-round."

Up and down Bundy Street more talk was going on. Nobody wanted to see the pier closed, and people were willing to do something about it—if they could only think of something to do.

"It takes money," said Chico. "A lot more than any of us have. All the donations we could give wouldn't put one wooden pile back in place."

"But we have talents," Flo argued. "And we can all find a little spare time. How about pooling our resources? You know what I mean—sharing the things we do best. We could have a carnival right here on Bundy Street, featuring Chico's Chili, Old Lu's flowers, my tamales, Tony's monkey, and . . . and we could ask the pier people to set up booths and do whatever they do best. We might even have some sidewalk artists . . ."

" . . . and balloons," added Caro. "Don't forget the balloons—hundreds and hundreds of them—and popcorn from the Mayan Theater. They make the best in the world!"

Flo's idea spread quickly through the neighborhood, and help came from unexpected places. There were two artists in the Oak Apartments who would be glad to help, and a man named Mr. Pagliana had an accordion that he agreed to play if Tony would set up tables in front of the Deli, where people could sit and eat their pastrami sandwiches.

The city agreed to close Bundy Street to traffic for a day and put up large signs that would read

119

PEDESTRIANS ONLY. Chico and Tony strung cords with little lights in the sidewalk trees and taped them securely to the sidewalks so no one would trip over them. When they turned them on at night, the lights flickered on and off like tiny fireflies in the branches.

It was the middle of April before all the plans were completed. The carnival was set for the first Saturday in June. Posters were distributed all over town that said, SAVE THE PIER! and there was a big article in the newspaper. The headlines read: *Bundy Street Gives Pier a Second Chance.*

By this time, the city of La Mirada had repaired the front portion of the pier where the damage had not been severe, and the shops there had opened again. But the broken end of the pier was still barricaded, starting with Mrs. Olivetti's Sea View Snacks, which still hung dangerously over the water and looked as if it was about to fall in. The City Council was meeting soon, to decide whether or not general repairs would be worthwhile. Tony said that everyone was watching Bundy Street. What happened on June 1 would show how much people really cared.

Well, Caro thought with satisfaction, they cared a lot! When June 1 finally arrived, Bundy Street was filled and overflowing with people. The sounds of music and laughter filled the air, and the good smells of popcorn, hot tamales, Chico's chili, and pastrami sandwiches made people sniff with pleasure. Flowers in pots lined the sidewalks and blue morning glories opened their faces along the walls and fences. The artists set up their stands and drew sketches of Bundy Street. They sold them so fast they had to start taking orders. The lady from the Candy Shoppe spun sugar in five colors—to go with the balloons, she said—blue, yellow, pink, lavender, and green.

There was no way that the Lindstroms could bring their horses, but they brought the red ticket booth with its sea nymphs and lions' heads and offered three tickets for the price of one. They also brought a tape and played it so that their end of Bundy Street would hear "My Darling Clementine" and "The Sidewalks of New York" all day long.

In the evening, when Tony turned on the twinkling lights, everybody stopped talking and went "Ahhhhh . . ."

And then, as if there had been a signal, the whole huge crowd began to sing, "Oh, my darling . . . Oh, my darling . . ."

It sounded like one voice, and the melody floated up into the night, saying to anyone who would listen, "We care. Oh, how we care!"

15
The Music
Plays On

Suddenly, it was summer, and school was out. That, in itself, was reason for rejoicing. But there was more.

The City Council made its decision. The pier would be repaired and the lower-level fishing deck rebuilt. Of course, those structures that had been completely destroyed would have to be built again by the owners—but there was some insurance, and that, along with all the donations that kept pouring in, would help. It was amazing, the Council announced, how much affection people seemed to have for the old pier.

But Caro didn't think it was amazing at all. Now there was going to be a celebration. Bundy Street and the pier people were getting together for a giant wiener roast on the La Mirada beach. It started early in the evening, so that everybody could enjoy the sunset. Tony and Chico and some of the other men built three bonfires, and each person got to roast his own wiener on a long stick. They ate them in buns with the catsup and mustard and sweet pickle relish dripping out the ends. Then they washed their hands in salt water and dried them in the warm breeze. Of course, there were big pots of Chico's chili, too, and trays of tamales, and white, fluffy marshmallows that turned golden brown when they were held over the embers.

Syl fixed one for Tien. He tasted it carefully because it was the first toasted marshmallow he had ever eaten. At first he made a funny face. Then he ran his tongue all the way around his lips and said the first English word that he had ever learned, "OK!"

Caro ate until she couldn't eat anymore, and then she helped Syl and Tien and Thu Anh build the biggest sand castle she had ever seen. When the sun went down and the sky grew dark, they looked up and saw the stars tracing ancient legends in the sky. Finally they walked along the beach, feeling the sand cool and wet beneath their feet and letting the water wash over their toes.

The tide comes in—the tide goes out, Caro thought. The sand shifts every time the water slides over it. It's still the beach. It's still a place where friends can meet and build castles in the sand. But it's a little different every day.

That was what change meant, she supposed. You didn't always plan it. Sometimes you didn't even want it. But it happened just the same. She thought of the time when the waves had broken down the walls of their castle and destroyed the tower. That was terrible—but only for a minute—only until they had started to rebuild. And the next castle had been even better.

She looked at her mother, sitting over by the fire with her head on Tony's shoulder. The new baby meant change. A lot of it. Caro shrugged. Good things could come from unexpected places. She would hold that thought. After all, if everything had stayed the same, she would never have met Thu Anh—Tien would never have talked—Syl would never have become her friend.

Maybe the baby would be someone special—someone who would make their family better than ever. Caro began to wonder if the baby would be a her or a him, and she felt a little prickle of excitement at the wondering.

God does answer everybody's prayers, she decided. But he answers them in the way that he knows is best. Sometimes he might have to say no, just like Tony did when Caro wanted to do something that wasn't good for her. But God didn't stop there. He helped you grow—he helped you change, so that you would understand what was right.

Thu Anh gave a little skip-hop that put her in step with Caro. But she didn't stay that way. Before long she was off kilter again. "It's because my legs are too short," she laughed.

Caro thought there was another reason. Everybody has a rhythm, she thought—kind of like a private heartbeat. She remembered the skater on the pier who wore a sign saying, "I carry my music with me." Everybody did that. The music was inside you.

"Every single person in the world is different," she told Thu Anh. "I think what each person does can affect the whole world."

Thu Anh looked at her in surprise. "Of course," she said. "Even if what you do is only a little thing. My father says, 'A sonata is as lovely as a symphony; a poem is as rewarding as a book.'"

Caro smiled. "Flo says the same thing, only it sounds like, 'It's the quality of the act, not the size, that counts.'"

She smiled again, but this time to herself. Being nice to Syl or bringing a flower to her mother or telling

124

Chico he made the best chili in the world—those were important things. Being yourself was important—knowing that you were part of God's plan—a unique creation who could love and give as no other person could.

A gentle breeze swept over the beach. Caro looked out beyond the sand and across the water. The waves were shimmering in the moonlight—rising and falling in a gentle rhythm of their own as they slapped softly against the new piles of the pier.

Caro reached out and touched Thu Anh on the shoulder. "Look," she whispered. "And listen." Thu Anh smiled and nodded her head.

"It is so peaceful . . . so beautiful," she murmured.

The two girls stood in silence, and Caro knew they were both thinking how different this was from the night of the storm when they had huddled together at Sinbad's. Caro lifted her head, feeling the moment of gentleness that reached out on the soft wind and caressed them both . . . like a feather from a sea gull's wing. It was a moment to remember the next time she felt lost or alone.

Voices rose, laughing, from the beach behind her. Softly, so softly, she heard the music from the carousel. But the greatest music was all around her—the sounds of life and living, the voices of people, all working together, each in his own way.

This was it, thought Caro. This was the way to fly. When you could see the beauty of a single moment, when you could feel love and joy and reach out with understanding, knowing that God needed you for what you alone could do. Then it didn't matter when the carousel stopped playing.

Your music played long past midnight when it was inside you and you could hear it forever.

MARILYN CRAM DONAHUE is a free-lance writer
and former teacher, who taught English as a second
language to immigrants. She has written two other
junior novels, *To Catch a Golden Ring* and *The
Crooked Gate,* and is now working on another book
in the Bundy Street Gang Series.